Praise for Lisa Samson

"Samson's quirky characters will have readers laughing, crying, and shaking their heads in disbelief, sometimes all at the same time. This uplifting read . . . will attract fans of women's fiction and especially works by authors Sarah Jio, Anne Tyler, and Alice Hoffman."

—*LIBRARY JOURNAL*
ON *RUNAWAY SAINT*

"At the same time funny and meaningful, this is a beautiful gem. . . . The characters shine from the page with amazing insight and reminders about what's important."

—*RT BOOK REVIEWS*, 4 1/2

STARS, TOP PICK! REVIEW OF
THE SKY BENEATH MY FEET

"Samson is bold as ever, exploring big questions through her vivid writing and memorable characters."

—*PUBLISHERS WEEKLY* REVIEW
OF *RESURRECTION IN MAY*

"Samson spins a convincing tale about the plans we make for our lives and how God often has other ideas. Well written and enjoyable, this title will appeal to readers who appreciate intelligent fiction with a spiritual element."

—*LIBRARY JOURNAL* REVIEW OF
THE PASSION OF MARY-MARGARET

"Quirk works; this is a deeply engaging book deserving of a broad audience."

—*PUBLISHERS WEEKLY*
STARRED REVIEW OF *THE*
PASSION OF MARY-MARGARET

"[A] staggering examination of the Christian conscience. [Samson] paints an emotionally and spiritually luminous portrait of a soul beckoned by God."

—*PUBLISHERS WEEKLY*
REVIEW OF *QUAKER SUMMER*

A Thing
of Beauty

Also by Lisa Samson

Runaway Saint
The Sky Beneath My Feet
Resurrection in May
The Passion of Mary Margaret
Quaker Summer
Embrace Me

A Thing of Beauty

LISA SAMSON

THOMAS NELSON
Since 1798

NASHVILLE   MEXICO CITY   RIO DE JANEIRO

Published in Nashville, Tennessee, by Thomas Nelson. Thomas Nelson is a registered trademark of HarperCollins Christian Publishing, Inc.

Thomas Nelson titles may be purchased in bulk for educational, business, fund-raising, or sales promotional use. For information, please email SpecialMarkets@ThomasNelson.com.

Publisher's Note: This novel is a work of fiction. Names, characters, places, and incidents are either products of the author's imagination or used fictitiously. All characters are fictional, and any similarity to people living or dead is purely coincidental.

Library of Congress Cataloging-in-Publication Data

Library of Congress Cataloging-in-Publication Data
Samson, Lisa, 1964-
  A thing of beauty / Lisa Samson.
    pages ; cm
  ISBN 978-1-59554-547-3 (softcover)
1. Actors--Fiction. 2. Blacksmiths--Fiction. I. Title.
PS3569.A46673T48 2015
813'.54--dc23

                          2014029934

Printed in the United States of America

14 15 16 17 18 19 RRD 6 5 4 3 2 1

For Ty, who never fails to encourage, support, love, and accept. You are an exceptional woman.

One

All the Nutty Bars in the world won't make this problem go away. In July, Jessica is coming out with a tell-all autobiography giving "her side of the story once and for all." She's apparently banking on the fact that I won't enforce the gag order placed upon her during the parental divorce proceedings, and she's right. I'll have to go her one better.

I don't want to do it, but she's given me no choice. The mother I divorced when I was sixteen won't be silenced, and when she makes up her mind to do something, consider it done. I can only throw my current privacy up in the air and hope bits of it come back down when this is all over. Deborah Raines has agreed to an exclusive interview with me a week before the book's release, and that will be that.

Simple, right?

But I need money. Because it takes some to look like you have some, and Deborah Raines and the world that watches her need to think I am doing better than ever. Nobody will follow up because nobody really cares. Kind of like that college diploma employers never ask to see.

So I do what I have to do: compose an ad and cross my fingers that someone out there will answer my call.

Four months and twenty-two hundred dollars could make all the difference.

Craigslist: Housing: Room for Rent.
Mount Vernon, $550/month

Room for rent with attached, private bath. And I do mean a room. A room with a door to the hall bath cut into its wall so all the renter has to do is come in the front door, walk down the hall to the second room on the right, close the door behind him, and that will be that. And nothing more.

Kitchen usage, not okay. Hot plate, microwave, and dormitory refrigerator in the bedroom, fine.

Washing machine and dryer, not okay. Bathroom sink, tub, and shower curtain rod, fine. Better yet, find a Laundromat.

Living room. Try not to even look at it on your way back to your room. Rent is $550 a month and you know what? That's a steal in this neighborhood, so any complaining and you know where to find the door. I'm not kidding.

And if I find you anywhere else in the house or the backyard (feel free to use the front porch to sit on if you must and bring your own chair, but don't just leave it sitting there for all time), I'll personally remove you from the premises because I didn't take kung fu purely for my health and peace of mind. But a woman doesn't need peace of mind to kick somebody's ass. Preferably not yours, but I'll do it if I must and not look back.

E-mails only.

After posting the ad designed to weed out anybody hoping to become my very best friend, and putting off any creepers with my bald-faced lie about martial arts, I lay my cell phone down on the kitchen table and begin outlining on a piece of graph paper the suitable space for a renter's feet to navigate. I am reminded of a marble maze with only one possible path, all doorways clogged, one place only, one place only. How great that would be to have a world of options stripped away, because with too much choice one can only stand still and gather as much information to make as wise a choice as possible. And there are too many choices, too much to know.

But this arrangement? I hold the graph out in front of me. This arrangement is a thing of beauty. I almost wish I was my own renter, my options stripped away. This seems like true freedom.

※

Fifteen minutes later I pedal beneath the dense March cloud cover spewing forth a chilled rain of paunchy droplets that splatter like paint over the lenses of my glasses and soak their chill into my bones. Bikes are nice, okay. In summer.

A pile of trash in the alleyway that runs down the middle of the next block tickles my peripheral vision, and I make a quick left. Checkin' it out, checkin' it out. You never know when you're going to find it. *It*. And don't tell me it can't be found in a pile of trash. I know better. The universe has a different set of values than we do. Case in point: the digestive system. It has a beauty all its own and doesn't care what anybody thinks about it.

Sifting through pieces of scrap wood, a couple of outdated countertop appliances, old towels, and just plain old junk, I expose piece upon piece, hope in my heart. Something glimmers down on the pavement, something small. A ring, perhaps? A diamond? Or maybe just something humble, a department store piece of costume jewelry.

"Hey, you right there! What are you doing?"

A woman stands silhouetted by the light at the entrance to the alley ten feet away. Her hands press into her hips and her high black heels stab into the cobblestone paving.

"You hear me?" she says with a shake of her blond bob.

"I just saw the trash. I'm an artist and—"

She bends down and picks up a bottle lying by a blue compact car. "Get out of here. This is private property."

It isn't. It's on the street, but it's not worth fighting over. The sparkle was only a piece of crushed soda can. I get on my bike and continue down the alley, away from the woman.

"Don't come back!" she cries, her words forcing themselves against my back as I speed up. There are other piles to find. More than there should be. The bottle whizzes past my head.

But I am shaking. Every time I go out, I think it might feel different. And every time it doesn't. Some days it's easier to ignore it than others.

I sleep for the rest of the day as the responses to my ad pile up in my e-mail's inbox.

❀

The next day I lock up my Schwinn to the bike rack at Begonia's Coffee Bizarre for my weekly outing, committing myself to warmth and human interaction. Not that the lady in the alley didn't have her certain brand of charminess. But here I remember what moving about life feels like. In the same manner as everybody else who's just doing her thing, I still have the skills necessary to frequent a coffee shop. I'm still capable of interviewing potential housemates.

After setting my tote on the lime-green ice-cream-shop table at the very back corner, I wipe my glasses clean on the hem of my black pullover, a hairy number that could easily be mistaken for a werewolf attack. I pull a hair tie from around my wrist and twist back into a bun hair that can only be described as a nondescript brown, okay, because nobody wants their locks to be compared to the water left in the bucket after a good mop of the basement floor. If you choose to picture it that way, however, you're close.

After all of this activity, I'm still freezing.

That's what they don't tell you in Hollywood when they expect you to look like a Halloween skeleton. They don't tell you how cold it is to be skinny. And they don't tell you how even once you leave that life behind, you can never, ever look at food the same way. Oh, you don't have to think of it as the enemy for the rest of your life, but you do have to remind yourself every time you pour yourself a glass of chocolate milk that it isn't.

When she bought the shop, Randi, the owner of this fine establishment, felt that Randi's Coffee Bizarre didn't have the same ring as Begonia's. So she kept it with no intention on opening day or any day, including today, of ever being called Begonia. I can't imagine any human less of a Begonia than Randi, who, dressed in leather—basically—and wearing a bright-red-and-black beehive hairdo, leans against the back counter. She glances up from the puzzle book she holds and peers over a pair of chrome reading glasses that would more accurately be described as goggles.

"Morning, Fia." Her musical voice greets me and she starts in on my latte, now on the menu as the Morning Buster, a twenty-four-ounce mug holding half-and-half, five shots of espresso, and two pumps each of caramel, chocolate, white chocolate, and coconut syrups.

This concoction made the front page of the *Star* ten years ago.

"Hi, Randi." I perch on one of the chairs at the counter. Randi takes no mind of my sweater.

"Miserable day, you know?" Randi asks. "Did you walk?"

"I finally got my bike out of the shop."

"Poor old thing."

"Poor stupid thing is more like it. Out of the past eight weeks, I was able to use her a whopping three days."

The bike shop guys are swamped now that pedaling is hip.

The steam wand sounds like it's sucking the brains out of the whole milk she poured into the stainless pitcher, so much so that I wonder if I'll end up in its vortex. "Is that thing louder than usual?"

"Yep. Costs two-fifty to fix and it still works, so . . . But about your bike. You might want to get something new, sister."

"And boring. I like that ruby ring you're wearing."

"My aunt's. Well, yeah, boring. That's usually the way it works, Fia. Reliable rarely comes in a flashy package."

She's right about that.

"If ever." I rest my chin in my hand and can't help but sigh. I'm not looking forward to the next hour. "So, okay, I've got people coming in to see me about the spare bedroom. Hopefully it will throw some business your way. And speaking of that, I know my tab is getting really long. I was wondering if there's anything I can do in exchange."

"Sure." Randi sets down four shot glasses beneath the four spouts of her red machine and pushes the buttons. The grinder metes out punishment on the beans, and who knew specialty coffee drinks came about through such violence? "So, are you looking for a male or a female boarder?"

"Hopefully male. I don't need a girlfriend."

"Guys are big and loud, though."

"Well then, he had better take off his shoes when he comes in the door. I really don't want to know he's there if at all possible."

"Hmm." She frowns. "Men are also more demanding, and he might feel like he has a right to have more of a say than he does. Like, his word should be 60 percent and yours only 40 or something."

Randi had two marriages go kaput and it's clear she has little hope for a third. "Better that than painting our nails together or having to ask if he wants in on the carryout order I want to make every single time. That would be a nightmare."

"I'll grant you that. Women can be a giant pain in the butt too," she says.

"Well, I am interviewing one woman this morning, however, because you just never know."

"What did you have in mind regarding your tab?" Randi asks as a sudden parting in the clouds sends in a ray of sun through the plate-glass front window to spotlight her hair. That is some *red* red, ladies and gentlemen.

"Some kind of mural in the hallway?" I suggest, almost praying for her to screw up her face in disgust at the suggestion.

Randi nods. "Like maybe a woman at an interview desk, men lined up for the privilege of being her roommate?"

I should ask her to beehive my hair before the first interviewee arrives. "Yep. Only the thought of that makes me want to throw up a little."

"Even after all the dates you go on, Fia?" She dumps the espresso into a large cylindrical mug with the words *Love Is All You Need* and a toothy cartoon rendering of the Beatles on the side. "Please."

"It's only because TV has gotten so bad lately. Especially if you don't have cable."

Randi begins pumping the sugary syrups into the mug. "I hear that. So how many interviewees do you have lined up?"

"Four. In fifteen-minute increments beginning at ten."

"Not going for the person who has a steady day job, I see." Randi's personal aesthetic bears no testimony to her practicality.

"Didn't think about that."

"Someone like me would never be able to make it to the interview. Well"—she pours the milk into the mug—"you can always schedule some more. And maybe you'll find someone today. There's always that."

"Yeah. Maybe I'll luck out."

She stirs the concoction with a tall teaspoon. "You know the way I think."

"'Everything happens for a reason, sister.'" I quote her, taking the drink as it's offered. I sip, feeling hopeful I might actually warm up. "And while I don't necessarily agree with your spiritual philosophy, I *always* appreciate your lattes."

"Well, if it has to be one or the other . . ."

A brass bell with the etchings of a Chinese dragon parading in a circle around it bounces like a Ping-Pong ball against the surface of the bright-yellow door as two metalheads enter. Dressed in their metalhead uniform of faded jeans heavily frayed at the bottom, band T-shirts (Slipknot for him, Between the Buried and Me for her), and, in the case of the boy, black Vans, and the girl, Doc Martens, they choose the table closest to the bathrooms.

"Hey, Phoebe. Hey, Brian," Randi says as they set up gamer devices.

I drift back to my table, sipping as I go. I started feeling old last year, the very first realization that I wasn't one of the younger crowd, and could no longer be misconstrued to be such, occurring at the Fourth of July fireworks when a couple walked past me with their hands in each other's back pockets and I wanted to gag.

But even that memory cannot hide that the latte is starting to work its homey magic and overtake the chill of the bike ride. It's hard not to feel cozy here in a place that's half genie bottle, half fifties ski chalet, with a wave of a fairy princess wand added in for good measure.

Throw in a little Mother Earth while you're at it too.

And there's never a speck of dust on all Randi's bric-a-brac. You have to respect a woman who's able to keep up on all her bric-a-brac.

So then. Five minutes until . . . I open up my graph paper pad and spot the first name on the list . . . a Mr. Weisenheim should appear. You can't make this stuff up, folks. After that, Ellen Reinbacher, then Bartholomew Hipschman.

What? Did someone kick a bus of German tourists to the curb or something? Then again, this is Baltimore.

Another man, scheduled for ten forty-five, was basically unintelligible when he left a voice mail. But as long as his rent money jumps the fences between his account and mine, I couldn't give a rat's ass whether I can understand what he's saying.

And that's it. I just need one out of four to work out. Good odds.

"Fiona," Randi calls. "Make it loud enough and entertaining enough and don't mind my eavesdropping, and we'll call the tab clear."

"You got it, Ms. Begonia."

Make these interviews a good scene for an eager viewer? That I can do.

The dragon bell slams against the door, and a man lumbers in wearing a black suit and a red silk tie with matching pocket scarf. His eyes, set deeply beneath hooded lids and fine gray brows, dart and come to rest on me. If that isn't a wig, well, okay, but then he's pretty bold to wear his pet ferret as a hat to a place that sells food.

Randi sighs, picks up her puzzle book, and leans back against the counter. But I see that little grin lift the corners of her full lips.

This should be a piece of cake.

I wave Mr. Weisenheim toward my table.

❋

After a particularly annoying interview with self-professed genius Ellen Reinbacher, Bartholomew Hipschman fails to show, so my second latte and I sit at one of the counter stools, and I doodle while Randi pencils in her Sudoku book.

"So, Fia," she says, looking down through the reading glasses held up by her nostrils, pencil poised like a harpoon over the puzzle. "Why are you renting out a room in the first place? Has it gotten that bad?"

"Jessica, I guess."

She turns her eyes up to me. "Really? Why would she want you to rent out a room?"

"Oh, she's never said anything about that one way or the other. I'm being forced into a preemptive strike."

"Over what?" Randi raises an eyebrow. "What's the dish?"

Randi is always interested in this gossip, not because any parents of mine are a concern of hers. That would be lovely if that were the case and maybe it is, but I'll never be able to know because Jessica and Brandon are movie stars.

"Both Jessica *and* Brandon called two nights ago," I say.

Randi holds up a finger, then picks up tongs and digs in the pastry case for a cheese Danish with chocolate drizzled across the top. She drops it on one of the many mismatched plates she finds at Sunday yard sales and sets it in front of me. "Spill it. That Danish comes from Peacock's so it better be good."

Oh. It's one of the most expensive bakeries in Canton. But this is Greektown. She could have gotten some serious baklava from Greektown Bakery for half the price.

But I don't say this because Randi loathes the fact that I eat sweets from the rising of the sun to the setting of the same and look about as robust as a punk rocker, and she does the same and looks as maternally built, despite the leather, as the Italian-Catholic lady at the dry cleaner next door who had eleven children back when she was doing that sort of thing.

I lower my voice. "Jessica called to say they're getting a divorce again, but not really."

She leans in and whispers, practically mouths the words, "Publicity stunt?"

"You got it."

"I don't know why they don't just go ahead and do it, Fia. I mean, really. They haven't actually lived together in well over twenty-five years."

Seven years after I was born.

The parents share one of those Idaho ranches Hollywood movie stars buy. Jessica resides in a large chalet-style house overlooking the river that borders their property. Brandon pretends he's some kind of trapper and lives on the back five hundred where it's rocky and rugged and elevated enough that he can sit on his front porch with binoculars and see who comes and goes from Jessica's digs. At least according to Jessica he does.

I find that hard to believe because nobody comes and goes from her digs. Also, Brandon hates boredom and, judging by his exploits, is not easily amused.

"Why the publicity?" Randi asks, giving in and plucking herself a pastry too.

"New film for Mom. Some movie where she's an aging writer who is also a new mother-in-law, and the new daughter-in-law happens to be the daughter of the boy in high school she never got over."

"Oh, gag. Is Gary Kenny the . . ." The Danish hovers in the air.

"Yup. *And* she's the new aging face for Rev-Up Cosmetics." I drop my forehead into the palm of my hand.

"What about your dad?"

"He said nothing about the divorce one way or the other in

his message. But he's working on some alien movie right now. And not the cheesy kind either."

She shakes the tongs at me, Danish still dangling between the jaws. "Well, it *is* Brandon Hume. One doesn't normally associate him with cheese."

True.

"The whole thing is on a sound stage in London. Poor, poor man."

"My heart bleeds," Randi says with a smirk.

One of the things I miss the most about acting is going to London all the time. I found as many excuses to be there as possible.

She grabs another plate for herself. "He staying at the apartment there?"

"Yup."

She shakes her head and *tsks*. "And here you are, interviewing people in my coffee shop to rent out a room."

"Yup."

"Divorce is a messy thing."

Extra meaning expands Randi's words. Because my divorce was an exception to the rule as most divorces go, and it caused a media sensation when it happened. But anyone with any deductive reasoning skills wasn't surprised when I divorced my parents at sixteen. I knew everything about everything, being a child star with too much admiration and too little real affection heaped on her like burning ice. And now only a handful of people know what happened to me once I left Hollywood.

"I'm still not getting why this has anything to do with you renting out that room."

"She's got a book coming out this summer, Randi. A memoir. A tell-all. About my youth, my divorce from them, everything from her perspective. She told me she pulled no punches and that the day of reckoning has come for all of us. 'We deserve to tell the truth of our lives no matter who it affects,' she told me."

"Meaning you."

"Yup."

"Still not sure where the rented room fits in, Fia." She cocks her head toward me. "Now, I know I'm not the Hollywood type and all that, but—"

"I've scheduled an interview with Deborah Raines."

"Really? Like, a real journalist type?" Randi grins. "Whoa."

Deborah Raines's first big interview was with Liz Taylor after her divorce with Richard Burton was final, and she's been conducting them ever since. She doesn't let people get away with pat answers and cheerful evasions. That's what I need. Someone serious.

I can't believe she said yes.

"Jessica's given me no choice. I won't go the rest of my life with the world thinking it was my fault. She gets away with the things she does because nobody will stand up to her."

"I can see that. But what about the rent?"

"I need the money to get myself fixed up. The hair, the makeup, a new outfit that the public has never seen before. Luxury transportation up there and a few nights at the St. Regis. It's going to cost a small fortune."

She picks her puzzle book back up. "I'll bet. But don't the networks pay for the travel expenses?"

"Not the kind I'm going to need to make the impression I want. And let's be honest, Randi, we all know who is doing who the favor here."

I turn to sit back down.

"Fia?" Randi calls.

I turn around.

"What if you don't do the interview?"

I shrug and shake my head. "Life as usual?"

"And is that so bad?" she asks.

Yes. Yes, it really is.

Two

Back at my little table, trying to forget Randi's question, I listen to Brandon's voice mail a second time. I'm gathering this movie is different, probably because he isn't playing a German. Brandon is German-Jewish, which explains why his amazing, blond good looks coordinate especially well with military uniforms. I don't know if he's even bothered to count how many Nazi roles he's performed, but I'm sure it's at least fifty. He won an Oscar nomination for his portrayal of Reinhard Heydrich, the infamous architect of the Final Solution to "the Jewish problem."

The only reason I bring this up is because the costume is folded neatly and framed, complete with SS lightning bolts, and hanging over the mantel in his den.

Who does that?

He attempted to make me believe he did it to "never forget." But really? I think it's okay to forget the Holocaust when you're sitting by the fire having a glass of brandy and listening to your favorite Beethoven sonata. In fact, I think you *should.* There are plenty of times throughout the rest of the day to remember the bad things of this world.

The next interviewee shows up at my table just as I shut down my phone.

Judging by the gentle looks and overall demeanor of this new interviewee, however, I'm reasonably sure he would not only refuse a Nazi role, but if, under pain of death, he was forced to play it, would immediately burn the uniform afterward.

Wait.

He'd probably disassemble it and fashion it into something for practical use. Like a pot holder, or a dog bed.

First of all, after conversing with Randi, he bought a cup of coffee for himself and a latte that he now hands over to me. Second of all, he asks how I am doing, and I can tell he means it.

"Trying to butter me up?" I ask.

"Is it working?" He sits down.

I take a sip and nod. "It's not hurting. That's for sure."

"I'm Josia, by the way. Y-E-U. Yeu. Last name."

"Fia Hume."

"Pleased to meet you. I was listening in on your interviews," he says. I roll my eyes and he laughs. "Takes all kinds, but some kinds are easier to take than others."

Unlike an actress with too much Botox, Josia is one of those men with an age ranging anywhere from thirty to sixty. I'd pencil him in between fifty and sixty, but only because his eyes tell me I should. Gray, like mine, his remind me of the benign cloud cover of the overcast days I love so much. The force of the sun is comfortably hidden but your bike ride isn't spent fearing a downpour any second. It's not going to rain. You know it. It doesn't even smell like rain.

"So what keeps you occupied, Mr. Yeu?"

"Josia, if it's all the same to you."

I like his hands. They're purposeful hands, hands that do things, I'm sure. He might actually be handy to have around the house.

"Okay. So what do you do?" I ask again.

"I'm a designer and a craftsman."

Nailed it.

He continues, "Or, if you prefer, I own a forge where I make doors, fences, fireplace screens, gates, and the like. And sculptures when the time permits."

"A blacksmith?"

"Partly, yes."

"Are you temperamental like a lot of artists?" Because I'm all too aware of what that kind of malarkey looks like.

His smile is like a splinter of sunshine, waking up the gray of his eyes. "Not a bit. I enjoy the temperament of an auto factory worker who only ever wanted to be an auto factory worker, a man who enjoys his job all these years later and likes to grill out and go bass fishing on the weekend. And . . . he loves dogs and has three of them."

Laughter bursts out of me before I can remember I *am* a temperamental artist.

Randi's head jerks up from her crossword puzzle, and a look, at once mystified and pleased, passes over her face.

"I'm an artist too, which is why I ask." Well, kind of. That's the plan, anyway.

"Well, that's just beautiful." He leans forward and places his hands flat in front of him on the table, then turns them upward. "Tell me about your art." By his tone, you'd think I just told him I successfully endeavored to save an entire village from starvation and he wants all the details.

"I . . . don't know, Josia. I spray-paint things I find. And sometimes I put together things I find."

"Always with things you find?"

"Yes. Or can get real cheap at that thrift store down on Howard. Know the one?"

"Oh yes!" He sits back in his chair and curls his hand around his cup. "The one that sells building supplies, furniture, and what have you?"

"That's the place. Have you been there?"

He shakes his head.

I almost say, "Well, we'll have to go over there someday." But . . . bite my tongue!

Maybe I should tell him to forget about the room. He's too nice and I might actually find him sitting in my kitchen. I don't want him in my kitchen. What would be next? The parlor? The dining room? Meals for two? Would you mind picking up the toilet paper for me on your way home from work?

That painted line down the hallway seems better and better.

Then again, due to the same niceness, sticking to the rules might be something that comes naturally to him. I need to know a little more.

"So, do you own your own forge? Because that would explain you being here at this time of the day."

"Yes."

Randi shakes her head with a grin and gives me one of those "Go on now!" waves.

"But," he continues, "I like to think of it as sharing it."

I'll bet he only eats foods that aren't genetically modified too. "You have other artists there?" I ask.

He nods, the same splinter of sunlight illuminating coarse white hair that was all once as red as the hair by the nape of his neck, hair that probably hasn't been barbered for a good six months or so. "Several. And apprentices too. But they come and they go for the most part. A lot go when they realize how much concentration and belief it all takes."

"Belief? That's an odd word choice."

"Not at all. They have to believe they can do it, that what I'm showing them is the way in which to forge iron."

"Why would they doubt?"

He shrugs. "Mostly because it's convenient, I think. I'm not doing anything new, that's for certain. They get there thinking they'll stand around and drink water and watch. But I throw them right in. It's the best way to learn."

Two more old men from the old guard table enter the shop with hair that looks like somebody trimmed it with pinking shears.

He shrugs. "I don't ask them to do anything I'm not willing to do myself. So it's not like I have them there for just the grunt work. We all do it all. That's the way it works at my forge."

"Well, as long as you don't try to do it all at my house, we should be all right."

He sits back in his chair. "Would you mind explaining what you mean?"

"The room rental?"

He briefly closes his eyes. "Ah, yes. All right. I should probably hear the house rules before we make any decisions."

And just like that, the interview turns around.

The fact of the matter is, a world of Weisenheims and Reinbachers waits to share my house, but I don't want them; I want a friendly man like Josia Yeu. It doesn't matter that I'll rarely see him; the thought of Josia being around my house feels like the best-case scenario, and I can't tell you why. He just feels like the walking embodiment of "this is the way life's supposed to be!" The man who might have coined the phrase "No man gets to the end of his life and wishes he had spent more time at the office." Only he came to that conclusion with plenty of time left.

I expound the rules, even digging the floor plan out of my tote bag and smoothing it on the surface of the table between us.

He nods as I talk, remaining calm as I explain.

"Why do you need this room anyway?" I ask, folding up the plan and tucking it back in my bag. "You don't seem like a room-renting type of person. Did you lose your home? Your forge is still in business, right?"

I see Randi grin.

"It sure is. I lived in a small house, a glorified shed really, on the property. Built it all myself, but goodness, it was beautiful. Do you like an Asian aesthetic?"

"Definitely. Clean. Pleasant proportions."

"Then you'd have liked my home. Unfortunately, so did the flames."

"Oh no!"

"I had only been living in it for a few years, but I felt very isolated. It was quite depressing before it burned down. In that regard, I suppose I can say it was for the best."

"What about your students?"

"They mostly have lives outside the forge. Except for Ted. He lives on the premises in a spare room in the main building. And I just haven't the heart to tell him to go somewhere else so I can use the room. He's a fine person, young still, with a really good heart. If you ever meet him, you'll see what I mean." He pauses. "Not that you'll ever meet him. But if you did."

"I see."

We both pause to sip. He smiles into my eyes, knowing I'm feeling the awkwardness of someone displaying an openness to which the other person is closed. Even in this, he assures me I can feel the way I'd like. No big deal.

He drains his cup, then sets it at the far right corner of his side of the table. "So all I want is just a room. I'm at the forge from before sunup to ten most nights. It's really just a place to lay my head. I think our needs will coincide perfectly."

"You want to see it first? I mean, most people would want to see it first."

He shakes his head and scratches his chin. "Doesn't matter. I can live anywhere there's an open door for me to enter, or at least a key is provided. You'll barely see me."

I feel a little disappointed. No nice conversations, no passing on the sidewalk?

Oh, he sits there so relaxed. One leg crossed over the other. Sipping his coffee again and looking out the window. He leans forward as he looks at the metalheads. Then he looks at me. "You've got to love young people these days."

"Why's that?"

"They advertise who they are. It's not like everyone dresses the same anymore. I'm glad the world's like that. Makes it easier to meet people where they are, don't you think?"

Meeting people where they are? Who wants to do that? "I guess so."

Is that his secret? Will I have to be known by this man?

Does he know me already? Something inside me cries out yes. Something else cries out no. I don't know who to believe or why it's even important.

But pragmatism wins the day, and I remember my home and all that resides therein and yes, Josia Yeu is perfect.

"Then again," he says, "the clothes may throw a person off too. That girl there? She might hate metal but only pretends to like it so her boyfriend will be happy."

"Or vice versa."

"Or vice versa! Yes! Good!"

We exchange phone numbers.

I walk him to the door, shake his hand, and remind him the move-in date isn't until next Tuesday.

He climbs into a large white pickup truck, older but beautifully kept (a good sign), and soon drives off, easy.

"Why next Tuesday?" Randi asks.

"I need a full five days to get the room in shape."

"That bad?"

"Well, you won't find me on *Animal Hoarders*, so I guess it's not as bad as it could be."

Randi lets out a low whistle. "Need help?"

"Nope. But I'd better get to it."

This is not going to be fun. The chickens always come home to roost, and one of mine is pecking at my screen door.

This interview with Deborah Raines should have been done a long time ago. Maybe I just needed a decade to gather the strength. I should tell the whole truth. What Campbell did to me. Jessica's nonresponse. But really, a perverted director and a young actress is an age-old story in Hollywood, and does anybody really give a damn? I don't think so.

As I pack up my things, a younger man hurries toward me from the front door. "I'm sorry I'm late," he says. "I realize it's way past ten forty-five."

Wait. Josia wasn't my ten forty-five?

Three

I place my tote bag in the plastic woven front basket of my rusty old Schwinn and pedal away from the Bizarre. The rain, now stopped, allows my tires to suck up the water in its grooves and spit it back out, providing a pleasant rhythm. I love riding my bike after a rain with its *shippy-ta-shippy-ta-shippy-ta* cadence accompanying my journey.

I should take a left and go directly home, but the thought of the task ahead of me forces my handlebars right. What was I thinking buying such a huge town house in Mount Vernon? What one woman needs that many bedrooms? But it was also the last big purchase with my acting pay. I'm not ready to give that up.

Already I'm thinking about my hair. That's going to be the first big change I make with the rent money. My investment account is at an all-time low, and as you might guess, I've been drawing from it over the years while I decide what I want to do with the rest of my life.

I'm still not sure what I'm going to do, other than clean that bedroom and bathroom.

Such high ambitions, Fiona.

Hey, it's better than a week ago. It's a step in some kind of direction. Forward, backward, I can't tell. But here's to something being better than nothing.

I pedal down Eastern Avenue, cut over toward the Inner Harbor, wing past Harbor Place and the tourist sites, take a left on Light Street, and continue on until I turn left once more onto Fort Avenue.

I'm reasonably sure there will be several messages on my answering machine at home from my mother, who'll want to make absolutely sure I understood our conversation the night before.

Sure, I can sum it up for you, Jessica.

"When *your father and I* divorce, it's pretend. When *you* divorce, it's for real, Fiona. It's time the world knows the truth of what you did to us."

She would look so beautiful saying it too, that thick, short hair that once held the golden light of a wheat field in the sun, now more akin to the light of the moon on the snow outside, barely coming to rest on sharp, broad shoulders sprinkled with the intriguing, tiny brown spots of older women who've been able to afford years in the sun. On Jessica it happens to be alluring. That impossible waist. Legs still slender and shapely. She'd be looking good in white pants and a red sweater, standing by the sliding glass doors in her feminine but tastefully simple home office.

"When are you coming back home?" she asks almost every time we speak.

"Back to what?" I ask. I never even lived at that ranch. Back means a hell of a lot more than Jessica wants to realize. Surely she realizes. She was there, wasn't she? Wasn't everybody?

I stop for a small bottle of chocolate milk at a convenience store on Fort Avenue and read an article by the cash register about rampant sexual abuse in the world of the child star. Wowee, the writers sure got the scoop with that one. They must have been sitting around for three weeks racking their brains for something earth shattering.

"Do you want that magazine?" asks the cashier, a woman in a red T-shirt with the words *It's not rocket surgery, people* across her buxom chest.

I shake my head and slide the magazine back into the wire rack. "No, thanks."

I head outside and tuck the chocolate milk in the basket.

The point is, Mom knew what Campbell was doing to me, and she not only kept me in the industry, she kept me on his show. At one point, hoping to be alleviated from the horror, I begged to live a normal life.

"What's normal?" she asked.

And now, pedaling as fast as I can toward the interim destination I have chosen for the day, I can't even pinpoint what normal consists of because surely this life does not fall into that category. I'm thirty-two, with no children, no career, an old house filled with Nutty Bars and junk. This can't be regular. Please, dear God, don't let this be regular.

I'm glad I ended up here, though, in this town. At least there's that.

I love the streets of Baltimore, and I look from side to side as I pedal, hoping to obscure visions of Jessica with views of little rowhouses and pots on stair steps, painted screens and sub shops, but nope. She's not to be denied.

How can I not hate her a little?

Can someone tell me how to do otherwise?

When I first heard Reba McEntire sing that horrific ballad about poor little Fancy, dressed like a tramp, made up like a harlot, then sent into town all by her young teenage self because this was her one chance to make it out of this godforsaken town, this godforsaken life, this godforsaken house—her one and only chance—I wanted to call the country singer and say how that song trivialized matters like that. That when it's true, it's nothing to sing about. I knew exactly how poor Fancy felt. Only my mother wasn't wasting away from some particularly consumptive form of cancer, wearing an old shirtwaist dress with a dime store pin on the collar held up by skin and bones. Jessica didn't have any such thing as an excuse for what she did. Oh no. She couldn't have had some reason that, however twisted, made a tiny bit of sense. There couldn't have been something there for a daughter to hold on to, some small peg sticking out on which to hang forgiveness.

And I'm supposed to tell the world this?

I don't know where I will find the strength.

❋

After a while, my eyes focus on the stone gates of Fort McHenry, and just the sight of them starts to relax my muscles. This is my thinking spot. This is the space in which I feel an anonymous ownership, as if the fort is mine, each brick, every last stone, but nobody knows it. And when I'm seen sitting on the walls, people just think, *There's a girl out there sitting on the walls*, but what they don't know is that I own the place.

I zip through the gates and ride toward the museum.

I haven't had a big change in a while now. I've been quite good at keeping that up since Jade left. Beautiful Jade, with the curly black hair that fell in his eyes. His eyes burned. Those burning male eyes that I find sexier than a thousand boy actors. We'd met at the Fourth of July fireworks downtown and stayed by each other's side when we both realized we were there alone.

Those eyes burned when he said three years later, "I can't stand it in here anymore, Fia. You're burying yourself yard sale by yard sale."

"But it's for my art. I use these things!" I yelled that day, about five years ago, when we stood in the one room he called his own, up on the third floor, his recording studio.

Two boxes of old purple tile I'd managed to score at a construction site sat against the wall near the door. He should have been congratulating me for getting it up there on my own. Instead, he raised his index finger and shook it. "One. I asked you. One place. One lousy room to call my own. And I walk in here and look. Look right there!" He pointed to the boxes.

"I just need a place for these things and I didn't know—"

"Know where else to put them? Geez, Fia!"

That night he left. He calls once a month to see how I am doing and once a month I tell him I'm doing all right, just the same, figuring things out a little more each day.

The last statement is a bald-faced lie. I know it. He knows it. I probably ruined my last chance for love.

He was a looker, all right.

I chain my bike to the rack near the visitor center, then skirt the main fort itself in favor of one of the outer walls, a pointed wall overlooking the Patapsco River. Fort McHenry is an old star-shaped fort, famous for being the place where "the flag was still there," as sung in "The Star-Spangled Banner." I've always loved Francis Scott Key just a little bit. So does my grandpa. He used to bring me here as a kid when I stayed with my grand-parents for summer breaks before I started acting full-time.

Few people come out to my wall here, but today, down at the water's edge, I see two teenagers going at it: kissing, kissing, kissing. They're a beautiful couple really, with their little ski caps clinging to the backs of their heads and their funky jeans and worn sneakers. The glittered waters reflect a sun now fully emerged from the cloud cover, and the trees are stippled with buds. My heart yearns a little. Not for a relationship, which sur-prises me, but just for beauty, even small, winking shards of the stuff, for beauty all around.

This world can be such an ugly place.

❀

The boy takes the girl's hand.

I'd never really had a boyfriend before Jade. Lots of dates, okay, and even boys I saw regularly but never committed to. My best friend, Lila, and I didn't need males tagging along to have a great time together. In fact, they kind of ruined things. No, they definitely did.

All males? Every single one? This is how preferences become issues, I suppose. Some women know how to pick them, and some women don't.

The little couple by the water has settled down, sitting and smoking cigarettes, his head in her lap, her playfully slapping at him, then planting a kiss on his lips. Something closer to the fort, to my left, nabs their attention. I follow the direction of their gaze.

A film crew has begun setting up.

I recognize the logo on the equipment. Charm City Radio Pictures. They've had a hit homicide detective show, *Charm City Killing*, for ten years running, and Baltimoreans, particularly those who live downtown, are always talking about a Charm City sighting.

They sure cast some sexy detectives. Even I have to admit.

This is my third sighting, and instead of running away like usual, I sit and watch from my perch as the crew sets up minimal lighting, dragging equipment from an oversized van. Jasper Venn, the famous director/producer who owns Charm City, pulls up in a beat-up black Honda sedan, climbs out with a stainless steel travel mug, and starts his part of his shoot by chatting it up with the grips.

The man is sexy, with gray hair that falls below his chin but stays back from his forehead.

After an hour in which I lose some interest and return my viewing to the water, two actors arrive, the female lead with her wavy auburn hair and Irish face and a hard-edged, sexy black man who, quite seriously, can work a camera like nobody I've ever seen. *Charm City Killing* is the only show I've ever watched with the same faithfulness a widow attends daily mass.

When they start to shoot, my heart begins to pound in a

rhythm I haven't experienced in a decade. And when I can take it no longer, I climb down from the wall and find my Schwinn. Time to roll.

Surely there is a way to do the work you do best and be healthy and happy. But if you're an actor, isn't that just impossible?

Please say yes.

Four

When I say I'm renting out a bedroom, I actually mean what was once the house-keeper's room. One small, mullioned window, its corner home for a spider with a quarter-size light-brown body, shines a gar-bled light down over stacks of my supplies.

The first step? Remove it all, every little bit of it, down to the smallest pieces of lint cowering by the baseboards. I should ride to the hardware store for a box of contractor bags, heavy duty and able to hold baby rattles, Fisher Price toys, four dust-dripping vaporizers, and who knows what else. I have seven cribs in here too, burdened by no foreseeable planning for their usage, but they're good cribs, antique, made of fine wood.

I was going to do a sculpture/installation-type piece devoted to babyhood. I gathered supplies from every other room of my house, each one devoted to a color. A lot came from the yellow room and the pink room and the blue room. I don't even know what I was thinking now. No picture comes to mind, no ideas. All I see are pieces of childhoods I neither remember nor particularly care about. Junk.

That's not true. I do care, but still haven't figured out why.

I could pitch it all in the backyard and make this easy, but I just can't. I don't want Josia to see an even more unruly backyard, the same jungle I'd hoped to make into something beautiful someday, clay pots filled with begonias and geraniums sitting on the patio by the iron chaise lounge that rests in the corner ready to be painted, at this point of decision, robin's egg blue. Three fountains, because I have pumps for three, one of them in the pool I found when I first moved here, a black, amoeba-shaped bowl just begging for koi, remind me that plans exist to be followed because if they aren't, they're just dreams, and if they're just dreams, fine, but at least admit it.

I could just drag the hellish host of debris up to Jade's studio. It's not quite filled. After he left, I tried to leave his room free of supplies. But there is a lot of purple junk out there on the cheap. Now the attic is full too.

Sitting down on the floor of the hallway, I evaluate. The crib ends and sides must be saved. For that kind of lumber to end up in a landfill is criminal. The other stuff? Now I can't even imagine what I could do with it. Seriously, this stuff looks like so much garbage I might just as well already be at the landfill.

Well, at least there's a firm line of demarcation between keep-it and trash-it.

I start taking apart what cribs are put together and haul the ends and rails to the hallway where I lean them up against the wall. Taking the cribs apart, of course, leaves me with screws and bolts and the iron grids upon which the mattresses would sit. (No, I don't have the used mattresses. A few standards still remain.)

The problem with collecting other people's junk is you just don't know what to do with it when you don't want it anymore. You feel bad about throwing it to the curb. It's too much trouble to sell. So you keep it around, knowing if you can't redeem it exactly, you've at least rescued it. Somewhat.

❀

Thank goodness it's March. Normally the lack of heat in every part of the house but my bedroom and the kitchen fails to appear on my gratitude list . . . when I remember to make one. But by four, my grimy hands wiping sweat from my forehead are most likely leaving streaks rendering me far from red-carpet ready. Definitely a "stars in real life" photo that's not exactly the Starbucks Shot or the Trader Joe's Capture. A little more raw and even more human.

See? She's a people too!

I drop the hardware into a paper bag and haul it down to my basement workshop, where I toss it on the already over-flowing worktable.

After three hours of labor, I've cleared less than half of the ten-by-ten space, but the maple plank flooring waits to be noticed once again, and will it be surprised when I actually bring in a mop and bucket, assuming I can find either, and swipe up the dirt. How is it I own so much and can never find what I need?

How does dirt find its way into old houses like it does? Sometimes I think it's the house itself, old and disintegrating by degrees, breathing out sighs of itself, sighs longing for a little bit of notice.

Thankfully, there's nothing personal to assault me here in this room. Every bit of this is stuff I've brought in since I moved from California eleven years ago. Imagine, a twenty-one-year-old buying one of the mansions on Mount Vernon Place.

"I had dreams too, you know," I whisper. Dreams of collecting the memories of good times, not dust, meeting new people who didn't know anything about Hollywood, not walking around with ghosts from my past, becoming good friends with locals, and having a neighborhood bar. Artwork—my own, of course, that people would be happy to buy—figured in too.

If I could ever decide what it is I really want to do with art. There are a lot of different kinds of artists. Maybe even this house, this mausoleum of detritus and rejection, is a work of art unto itself.

Oh yeah. Definitely that.

I work steadily until the hour of seven thirty renders it too dark to see and the boxes have stacked up outside on the patio.

Rain tonight too. Beautiful.

An adult would have checked the forecast.

But now it's time to quit. Time to flip on my bedside lamp, eat a sandwich, drink a glass of chocolate milk, and see if anyone on The List is looking for a connection.

Will I be happy just to fire off a few e-mails filled with brash, sexy talk, like frayed lines from a bad movie? These men on the other end of the Internet are so prone to respond to what I've typed into my insignificant little cell-phone keyboard. I've stopped asking why that is. Because I know.

When Jade pulled open our front door for the last time, a friend's pickup loaded with his equipment, a backpack carrying the majority of his personal possessions hanging by the top strap from his fingers, he said, "Nobody's enough in and of themselves, Fia. What we carry makes all the difference in the world. And your load was just too damn heavy. Get rid of it. At least some of it. For your own sake if nobody else's."

That wasn't very nice, was it?

Five

I wake up the next morning to another dreary March day in Baltimore. I slide up and out of my bed, the quilt covered in clothing I justify by a low heating bill. No need to dress for the day since I never took off my jeans and sweater.

I jam my feet into a pair of slippers I found at a yard sale for a dollar—much too big, but the socks keep them on—and head down to the kitchen and the instant coffee awaiting me. It doesn't taste very good, but it's so much more straightforward in the preparation than having to fool around with one of the coffeemakers.

The digital clock on the *plugged-in* microwave, as opposed to the two that aren't, says 10:00 a.m.

I can't believe I slept this late.

On the kitchen table at which I eat, my bowl, plate, knife, fork, and spoon await. The other table, a sort of desk for collecting mail and small appliances, is shoved into the corner in front of a surprisingly empty built-in corner cabinet. I turn on the faucet, water drumming against the bottom of an old aluminum pot I took off Randi's hands when she got her new set. I turn the dial on the only burner that works on my gas range, the only burner because what kind of repairman wants to come into a place like this? A decent person wouldn't even allow a repairman to come into a place like this, God forbid the hot water heater ever goes out. The Baltimore Gas and Electric man might never get out of the basement.

But I know that when inspiration hits, it hits, and every single thing in here has an idea attached to it. I only have to remember it, write it down, and use it someday, and it will all make sense. I can never seem to find a pen, though.

After my coffee is sufficiently distributed in the boiling water, I take a seat at the table. I love my 1970s captain chairs. They spin. They roll. They make one's meal a more dynamic affair. I can view the room 360 degrees and never remove my derriere from the nubby fabric striped with autumn's hues.

In a copper bowl, breakfast awaits in a choice of packaged rectangles. Granola bars, cookie bars, rice cereal treats. I tear open a pack of Nutty Bars and pull the chocolate-covered waffled goodness from the cellophane wrap. My teeth close over the first inch, and I snap the bar down and away from my mouth. Little Debbie never grows old. The woman knows how to keep it going on. And she hasn't had one stitch of plastic surgery as far as I know.

❋

By noon the room is halfway cleared.

I could have been further along, but I found a large deli salad container filled with a ball of fabric and lace that, upon its unfurling, revealed itself for an antique christening gown. I have no idea when I bought this or how it ended up in the native habitat of potato salad, but it's been at least six years since I stopped going on crazy buying binges worthy of an ex-child star. I can only imagine myself in some antique shop, buying willy-nilly whatever took my fancy. Funny how the rings of supplies reflect my investment account. Snuggled to the walls lies the good stuff; in the middle ring, basic thrift store; yard sales next; then closest to the door, street discards.

The fabric of the gown feels softer than it should, the fine cotton lawn flowing between my fingers. Who was this baby? Boy or girl? Is the child old now, or even dead? Somebody cared, obviously. Enough to have the child baptized. I mean, is that what caring parents do? I don't know.

I giggle, imagining Jessica and Brandon standing up front in a cavernous stone church, statues lit under the chin by winking candles in red cups. They only took me to church when the drama of it all would appeal. Jessica would make sure to wear a lace mantilla for funerals, Brandon a tasteful gray suit or a blue blazer with freshly pressed khakis, a white shirt, and a school tie for baptisms or weddings.

It's time to get a little lunch and interact with that one requisite person a day so that I'm not completely alone in my white stucco world, held in by the brick of the walls and cut off by the Ionic pillars of the front porch. The balustrade up on the roof and the urns at the corners want to hold me underneath their watch, but as long as I go to the Bizarre, Subway, or my grandfather's, they cannot imprison me.

I hold my hand out the back door, happy when the highly local weather report says, "The sweater is all you need." So I flip off my slippers, shove my feet into my red biker boots, promise myself I will take a shower in the evening and not sleep in these clothes, then proceed to the marble front hall where my bicycle leans against the handrail of the left leg of the double staircase leading up to the gallery above.

The staircase is what sold me on the house, the curves mirroring each other like the harp motif on a brass music stand. The dust has collected between the finely turned posts and the soft white paint is chipped, but the risers still glow at their centers, polished by my feet every time I head to bed and come down the next day to face the world.

I figure I'll take my feet today. The Schwinn looks extra bedraggled after our big day yesterday, and I'm glad for the exercise. When I left California, I was fit and strong. Pricey rehab will do that for you. Now, well, I don't care so much. But who wants to become decrepit? Not me.

Soon I'm sitting in a yellow Subway booth eating a meatball

marinara, double sauce and white American cheese, and if you throw a couple of extra meatballs on there I won't say a word. Pat always winks and adds two more. But no more than two.

A message comes in on my phone from Jack, one of my regulars off The List, a place for an escort to catalog her services.

I provide entertainment, still. Just of a different sort. I let men pretend they own a part of me with their fees, but they don't because I don't let them go all the way. Close. But not all the way. That's why I'm under the list headed Barely Platonic.

Jack lives in a rehabbed rowhouse in Fells Point. Even though he's a structural engineer and travels half the time, an artistic eye and a knowledge of furniture design have enabled him to make an eclectic apartment from mostly thrift stores and Goodwill. I tell him he should have been a designer and he laughs, but the smile that lingers is pleased.

Jack is different from the other dates I get off The List. I'd want to be his friend if our arrangement didn't need to exist. But it does. So that's that.

How soon can you be here, Fia? he asks by text. Jack recognized me the first time we met up, and I didn't deny it like usual. He truly didn't seem bowled over by that fact, and I knew this could be a regular thing. He was educated and kind, and while maybe not Hollywood rich, he was doing fine by the standards of the real people of this world. More than fine.

I picture him sitting on his rooftop deck, watching the business of Baltimore below him: bicycle commuters, old ladies stiff-legging it up the sidewalk wearing rain bonnets and car coats, people parking along the street to run into the church across the corner, and occasionally, mourners piling into limousines at the funeral home across the street. His blondish hair is probably still wet from his shower, and the rest of the water that sluiced down over him and clung to his golden skin in a bathroom the size of a linen closet has been soaked up by the luscious bathrobe he always orders from the same catalog company in Portland, and always in the same color. Ivory.

"Why not white?" I asked him three years ago when we first entered into our arrangement.

"It's too dicey," he replied. "I hate anything that collects dirt."

So you know right away he's never been up at the old homestead on Mount Vernon Place.

I check the time in response to his question. *Forty-five minutes.*

Fine. I'm not heading out of town until tomorrow. I'm taking the day semi-off.

I'll have to shower at your place.

No prob.

So I head home, hop on the Schwinn, and pedal through the remaining lunchtime traffic pulsing down St. Paul Street, then whiz by the Harbor Place Pratt Street pavilion, past the Power Plant and all the people making their way in and out of B&N and the Hard Rock Café, two establishments I've yet to enter. B&N because I have a little book shop in my neighborhood with a great art section, the Hard Rock Café because I avoid anything that smacks of Hollywood. Do they have to take over the world? Is millions of dollars a picture not enough?

Once past the major piers—one leading to the aquarium, another to a tented music venue—I continue on toward Jack's. I finally stand before his door. Number 1117.

All right, then.

I knock and ten seconds later he answers. Jack is a prompt person who, when something needs doing, does it right away. For this reason, his spare time is free and light because his mind is clear. His attraction to me can be explained by the old adage that tells us opposites go together.

He sweeps his arm inside and I follow it. "Want some lemonade?" he asks.

"And a game of spades?"

"Let's do it, Fi. I'll be right back."

And he will be. Jack always does what he says he'll do.

My studio in the basement calls. Why I chose this spot when I had sixteen rooms filled with light and beauty, why I felt the need to put it down here, I still can't say. Judging by how well I've done as an artist, I might deserve even less, but then that would banish me out to the old well house. The spiders there might not welcome that.

Instead of remaining in the dungeon of creative pursuits, I walk out into my backyard. It had been a beautiful backyard when I bought the house, a bit of magic and fancy with its brick patio and stone path meandering through lush flora and cherry trees. It's hard to even imagine now what that garden looked like, really looked like. And I know I can never go back.

One of the cherry trees has died and the rest have stopped blooming.

Even if I took the time to pull out all the growth, most of the plants in the border gardens would be dead. It would be a different garden in the same place.

But the earth remains, and I can take comfort in the making of a new garden someday, a garden completely my own. I would have flowers in a rainbow of colors only heaven has beheld. And butterflies would gather and crickets would scrape out their tunes. That is what I would do.

I don't apologize for it either.

The breeze of early spring shuffles across my shoulders as overhead the sun is busy in the middle of setting. I hold my arms against my rib cage and will myself to remember that garden. Remember it, Fia.

Because spring is here, you see. And while the house is overwhelming me, perhaps I can tackle this square of earth I've borrowed until my time here is finished.

❀

The night comes on again, and I know that I could pull out my cell phone and rustle up a date online, but I've had enough social interaction for one day. In the final box from the maid's room, I found a treasure box of children's books, most of which I remembered from my own childhood.

One of the only redeeming qualities in a childhood home/ homes run by two movie stars is that both of them loved to hear themselves talk. It took Jessica three times as long as the average parent (two words never uttered together on behalf of Brandon and Jessica) to tell a simple story, like how at least three of the gas pumps at the Shell had red baggies covering the nozzles, or what it was like to have dinner with Frank, Mia, Elizabeth, and Richard at some club in Las Vegas.

Brandon, however, made reading aloud a grand performance. I'd snuggle up against him in our fabulous living room in Vail, tucked up against his side, sipping on a chocolate milkshake because we loved chocolate milkshakes, a fireplace glowing with a blaze that would see three Eskimo families through a winter, and his voice with the tones of a warm bowl of your favorite soup reading the words of Dr. Seuss or Richard Scarry. From his lips to my ears, each word drew my tender heart toward him.

After eating a packet of Nutty Bars, I mentally cast about for a suitable reading spot, then lay the books aside.

Six

Today Josia arrives. He didn't ask to sign a lease and I didn't offer, so at least we can be free to change the arrangement if and when it's necessary. I asked him about it when he called to make sure it was still a go from his end.

"Indeed, yes, Fia. I would never want you to have me around if you didn't want me to be there."

"So if it doesn't work, you'd move on?"

"I would."

"What if *you* want to move on?"

He laughed. "Hasn't happened so far since I've been living out in the big world, but I suppose there's a first time for everything. However, I don't foresee a problem. I'm happy to stay within your parameters."

"Okay. Good."

"It'll be all right. You'll see."

Josia, I can tell already, has a way of helping you realize that what he says makes perfect sense. I can't imagine him being the type of father who guilt-tripped his kids. If he even has any kids. I hadn't thought to ask, but hopefully I'll remember at some point.

Mug of instant coffee in hand, I inspect what I've done over the past week. The bedroom looks good. As good as it can at this point. It needs a coat of paint to cover years of scuff marks on the wall, and some of the woodwork has been damaged and needs replacing. But I scrubbed away any grime I could.

The bathroom, however, needs an overhaul. At least the plumbing works, but the fixtures were installed in a redo back in the fifties. The tile walls are cracked, some of the white rectangles missing altogether, and the flooring, with its octagonal tiles, is half gone, the rough subfloor exposed. The only window, which matches the one in the bedroom, is cracked as well, but how do you fix a mullioned window? Thankfully, it isn't broken out.

But at least it's as clean as I can make it.

I should probably charge him less. But I'm willing to wait to see his reaction before offering. Who knows what his little place was like? Sounds like little more than a glorified shed. What would a blacksmith know about building? I don't know these things, but I imagine there are not a lot of overlaps between a carpenter and a blacksmith.

Eleven a.m. and a knock thumps on the front door, proving that at least the house is still solid.

I yank open the heavy door, the light from a perfect spring morning and the clear, mellow air of the same entering before Josia does. "Come on in."

"You sure?"

He's an easy sight this afternoon in jeans, which are now relaxing after surviving the stiffer years of youth, and a red flannel shirt that looks fresh out of a package. He smells good, the steam of a recent shower still clinging to his skin. His hair seems even whiter out there in the sunlight.

"Yes. Really. Come in before I change my mind."

He steps onto the white marble floor and sets down the only thing he is carrying, a large frame backpack with a bedroll and pillow crowning the armature.

"Wow." He looks around. "This is beautiful."

"It was."

"Well. I guess beauty is in the eye of the beholder."

"It's so junky." Why does everything that once was good eventually go bad?

He waves a hand. "Oh, that. That's nothing."

Nothing?

"Really. It's all about what it was made to look like in the first place. And this place was made to be beautiful. It was beautiful at one time. Nothing wrong with it that I can see."

"Okay . . ."

He points to plasterwork of water lilies on the wall painted over many times since it was done years ago. "A local artist did that," he said. "He employed bright colors, made the walls happy with his work. But, as you can see, it doesn't remember that. It's just a white wall now with some floral relief. Not that it isn't pretty, you see. But . . ." He shrugs.

"Just not how it was made to be."

"Yep. It's a beauty, though. One of the prettier homes." He looks up the left staircase to the gallery above. Portraits really ought to hang there. "Is my room upstairs?"

I shake my head. "Back down the hallway there to the left."

"Should we go there now?"

I hug my own arms. "Might as well get it over with. Follow me."

My house is deep. Going down the hallway, we pass the living room, then the large formal dining room to the left. On the right are several closed doors. The first leads to a library, the second to the small hall bathroom with the crumbling floor, the third to Josia's room.

"What are all these cribs for?" he asks as we pass them.

"I wanted to do an art project with them. I tossed almost everything else, but some of this wood is good stuff."

"I'll say. Walnut right there, and cherry. Birch too."

"Yes."

"What were your plans for them?" He runs a sensitive hand over the carving on the walnut crib. "So pretty."

"It's been so long. I don't even remember, Josia."

We enter the room. He looks around, hands now in his

pockets. "Good. It's small. When I saw the house and how grand it was, I was hoping I wouldn't be in one of the family bedrooms. Maid's room?"

"Yes." I point to the bathroom door. "Private bath in there, although it isn't much."

He enters. "Nice tile!" he calls. "You mind if I replace the broken ones? Free of charge, of course."

"Do whatever you'd like." I follow him in. "I scrubbed the tub, but I know it doesn't look like it."

He runs a hand over the lip of the clawfoot tub. "I know how this stuff works. You can scrub and scrub and scrub, but sometimes you just have to forget about the stains and cover it up with some fresh porcelain."

"You can do that?"

"Yes. You just have to get off as much of the grime as you can and then go from there. Some stuff is just never coming off, but it's really okay to seal it in if you're okay with knowing it's there."

"That won't bother me."

"Me either. I kind of like it, Fia. Better than throwing everything away. Much better. People throw things away too much these days."

"Obviously I don't have that problem."

"See? It's not as bad as you think, then."

Perhaps.

"So is the backpack all you have?" I ask.

"I've got a cot in the truck I'll bring in, just a camp cot for now. I'll wait to bring a bed in after you decide if I'm allowed to stay or not." He laughs.

Josia's laugh is better than any drug I ever took in the olden days of motion pictures.

"Do you need a coffeemaker or a microwave?" I ask his back as it retreats down the hallway toward the entry hall.

"That would be great!" he calls over his shoulder.

As he brings in his cot, I dust off a Mr. Coffee circa 1982 and a Hotpoint microwave with actual dials, not a digital pad. I like the chrome on these things.

He's delighted as, once back in the bedroom, he takes them from me. "Good! I love these old things."

"I've tested them. They still work."

"Do you have a little table I could set them on?"

Do I have a little table? That's funny.

"I'll be right back."

Ten minutes later, using the forest green card table I procured from one of the upstairs bedrooms, he sets it up. "And I was wondering if you mind if I threw on a coat of paint in here, just to spruce things up a bit as they say."

"Feel free to do whatever you'd like, as long as our agreements are followed. Which, just to clarify. If you don't see me in the hallway, like, actually *in* the hallway, just don't talk to me because you can't help but walk by the kitchen, and I really don't want to have to be mean about things."

"I understand. No problem. Where's your bedroom? Just so I know how quiet I have to be when I come in at night."

"Not quiet at all. Don't worry about that. I'm up in the far back right corner of the house on the third floor. You could play a trombone down here and I wouldn't hear it."

"Good to know. Do you want to approve any changes or repairs I make?"

"I trust you. You have to live in it. You'll make it good for you. And I think I can reasonably assume you're not some horror movie weirdo who's going to paint everything black with some ghastly spider mural or something that lights up when you flip on your black light. Correct me if I'm wrong."

He howls. "Oh, you've got my number!"

"Some of us just have the gift."

He begins opening the cot. "Well, thank you for your vote of confidence. Of course I'm not going to do anything that this home cannot accept with beauty and grace. I like to respect the vibe of a house. Each has its own, don't you think?"

"I do."

I suddenly change my mind and blurt out, "And you can use the backyard if you want. It's not very, well, kempt, out there, to say the least. But there's a patio, and if you want to bring in a lounge chair to sit outside or something, be my guest."

"Good. That sounds agreeable. I'm an early bird and on nice days a bowl of cereal always tastes better outside."

I'm sure he's right about that.

I arrange my feet to face the door. "I haven't eaten out there for years, but anyway, feel free to use the space however you see fit."

"Can we see it now?"

"Yes."

We head back out into the corridor. I point to a door opposite the direction from which he entered the house. "That leads directly outside."

"So I don't have to desert the designated path."

"Pretty much."

"Good. If rules are rules . . ."

I turn the latch, grab the knob, and pull, only to feel the door catch. "I haven't gone through this door to the patio in years. I've always used the kitchen door."

I turn the latch once more, thinking maybe it's actually been unlocked all these years. And, true enough, the door opens.

You can feel very safe all the while not being safe at all, can't you? I realize.

"Well, looky there," Josia says, pointing at the lock. "That's an easy enough fix."

True enough.

"Feel free to go on outside," I say. "If you don't mind being your own tour guide, I have work to do, and oh"—I dig into my pocket for the key I had made the day before—"here you go. Welcome to Mount Vernon Place, aka *The Cave of Wonders.*"

"Ha! I love that movie."

"Me too."

I wait for him to recognize me. The seconds pass. But he just stares back at me. "Are you okay?" he asks.

"Yes. Yes, I am."

I put forward my hand and shake his again. This time he enfolds mine into both of his. "Many thanks for the opportunity, Fia. I think it will all work out just fine."

Because you'll make sure it will? I ask inside my head, hoping the answer will be yes. Hoping the answer will be, "Of course." Longing for him to say, "I'm here now. Everything will be all right."

But he doesn't say this. And why should he? He's here to rent a room, not work miracles.

I head toward the kitchen.

"Fia!" he calls.

I turn to face him. "Yes?"

"I, on the other hand, have an open-door policy. If ever you need me, just give me a knock."

Of course he'd say that.

Seven

At eleven, I enter the house. Darkness enfolds me as I shut the door behind me and amble back to the kitchen. A golden light surges from underneath Josia's door onto the wood floors. I left at nine for a date from The List, a quick call for some human interaction and a cocktail. I can't imagine what Randi would say about the chances I take. And if I don't tell her, who am I going to tell?

Definitely not Josia. It's not that he's naïve, but there's a certain innocence about him I'd rather not taint.

With no overhead light in the room, I'm not sure where the light is coming from; however, it's none of my business unless I choose to make it thus. I know he didn't find a lamp from one of the rooms here because he told me he wouldn't go off the designated path and I believe him.

I throw my key ring on the administrative kitchen table and decide I might as well listen to my voice mail.

"Hello, Fia. It's your mother. Have you seen the tabloids? It's fast and furious now, but don't you worry about a thing. Everything is per usual here in the canyon."

That's what Jessica calls their compound, "the canyon," because having a thousand acres isn't enough. She has to lay claim to the entire geographic region.

One day my mother might really fall in love, and those divorce rumors coming from her side of the canyon will be more than rumors. But fat chance of that! Why she's content to let her life remain the same year after year is something I've yet to figure out. She does love to act, though.

I do too, but I'm not sure if it's because it was the only thing I was actually good at. Which is why my fall was that much more of a disappointment to the world and everyone around me. It's one thing if you're there for your bra size and your ability to be cute, or to shock, and you can deliver a line in a manner that doesn't embarrass you or anyone associated with you. When you fall, people aren't surprised. They feel bad for you, sure, but the fall isn't as steep as it might have been had you been a person of real talent, so they don't necessarily feel deprived.

I made them feel deprived.

No more roles from Southern literary fiction brought to life under my touch. No more moments as the bright spot of acting in an action film. No more portrayals of young British ladies quietly and torturously repressed. I loved being that little glimmer of hope that a young actress really cared about her craft.

But then, I didn't care much about anything else, and playing other people isn't enough to teach you how to act in your own personal melodrama. In fact, it just widens the scope of your choices, making it impossible to decide anything for yourself.

So when I get Jessica's messages, I can't just pick up the phone and ask, "Why? Why, why, WHY are you telling me this? What about the letters D-I-V-O-R-C-E spell 'free access anytime' to you?"

The next message is Jessica again. "Oh, and about the book, I know you're going to be upset. But there's just nothing I can do about it. The truth is the truth, you know. And even despite all that you did, I still love you. Which is a miracle on my part, I think."

Jessica's call reminds me that I've got to get moving on the preparation for my interview. I look weak and anemic. Maybe I need to bike more. Do some push-ups. Something to give my arms some body.

The next message is from Randi, giving me some ideas she came up with for the Bizarre. And what would I think of maybe putting together a 3-D sculpture arch for the inside of the doorway?

"I'm thinking some of those interesting items you're always finding, Fia." I hear the whir of the bean grinder in the background. "Somehow welded into an arch. Still not sure what color I want you to paint it, but I want it uniform and I want it bold. See ya!"

Red. I see it red.

So, nothing worthy of a blurb in the *Weekly World News*, and I'm grateful. I pull out the bottle of grape soda I bought at the Shell on my way home, heat up a can of soup, and head upstairs. I secretly hope Josia's door will be open and he'll see me in the shared space of the hall, but it remains the same. I turn at the end of the hall and the light in his room goes out.

Oh well.

It's just me, grape soda, and the latest book on the three steps to happiness and productivity.

I want somebody to write *this* book: the three steps you need to take before you're ready to take any step at all. But so far I haven't found anything like it.

❀

Three a.m. and I feel like somebody put diodes all over me and jolted me back to consciousness. I sit up, trying to remember if it was a dream that summoned me, but nothing comes to mind. Usually you remember those jarring dreams that force you from their surreal, slanted corridors, and I don't recall anything. In fact, I had been enjoying one of those rare, black sleeps that only asks to take you along for a simple ride of rest: Lie back, don't worry about a thing. I'll take it from here.

When I say awake, I mean decisively awake, the kind of awake that forces you just to throw back the covers without thinking. Which, when I do, allows all the cold air of the room to come whooshing in around my skin. My underwear does nothing to ward off the chill. I didn't fall asleep in my clothing, not after meeting up with Polo guy who would probably drink that cologne if he could. Heck, maybe he does.

So I grab the woolly mammoth sweater and jerk on a pair of yoga pants. After shoving on my slippers, I make the trek downstairs because I don't know what else to do at three in the morning other than check my phone. I sit on the bottom step and see what's happening online. Every so often there's a mention of me, usually filled with pity that someone given all the blessings I was given—wealth, talent, opportunity, and beauty (amazing what Hollywood can do to make an otherwise "regular pretty" look outstanding)—would throw it all away. That if all that didn't make her happy, nothing would.

Win an Oscar and you're likely to come up every so often, I guess.

I don't even know where I put that statue now. Best Supporting Actress. It's not an easy category to win because that's where so many of the really talented women, who might not be sexy and beautiful, end up.

Who in the *hell* misplaces an Oscar?

I figure I might as well make a cup of tea, so I proceed to the kitchen.

The light is back on in Josia's room and a power tool whines, adding sound waves to the light waves that spill across the floor. I stand still, hardly breathing, wondering what he's doing in there, knowing he's up to something.

"*Just knock,*" he said. But I can't. I'm not sure he'd hear me anyway.

Not even twenty-four hours and he's already living up to his word of making some improvements. I pictured him rolling on a coat of paint. Sure. But this is a tool thing, and tool things mean a lot of work, and we only do a lot of work on things that are important to us.

Maybe this house is important to him.

Or maybe making things beautiful is important to him, and where he is doesn't matter in the least. Or it all matters.

The man is a mystery.

The next morning around nine, after grabbing another few hours of sleep, I stand at his door. I'm pretty sure he's already gone to the forge. That kind of unoccupied silence seeps out.

Who sleeps for three hours, is up by 3:00 a.m., and keeps on going as if that is the start of his day? Maybe it *is* the start of his day. Maybe he doesn't need a lot of sleep. Maybe he loves being awake, awake, awake because so many wonderful things are waiting to be accomplished in the light of full consciousness.

Sounds like hell to me.

I wait another minute, still no sound. Do I open the door? Do I see what he's done in there?

What a violation of his privacy.

Again, *"Just knock,"* he said. Is that all I have to do? Do I wait for a more formal invitation or just take his words at face value?

I remember the list of parameters I've given him and decide that fair is fair. I cannot expect more of him than I'm willing to give myself, even if he is capable of handling more. Isn't that right?

Isn't that the way it works?

Time for my instant coffee. I assemble the beverage, then head to the patio. All the boxes from Josia's room have been stacked neatly against the house, and the old iron chaise now faces the overgrown garden.

He's right. This would make a nice place to eat cereal. If I ate cereal.

But I can drink my coffee here. So I do. Even in the chill of a March morning, this is extra nice. The coffee feels hotter and more delicious. More real than in the kitchen. More special. Like coffee when you're camping, or what a cup must have felt like when you were about to jump back aboard the Conestoga and continue the trek west.

Maybe I should take a clue from Josia and keep making things better. I could go through the boxes, sorting all the items into keep and discard piles. But how am I going to get rid of the stuff I don't want?

That's always been a major problem. You can have a bunch of items you've let go of in your heart, but if you've got no way to get them out, like Dorothy's shoes, "There they are, and there they'll stay."

After heading inside, I rinse out my cup and trudge upstairs for a shower. In the hallway a note hangs taped to one of two crib ends stacked together near his door. "Would love to use these ends. Hope you don't mind. I think you'll like the result. I won't use them until I know you're okay with it. Just leave a note and let me know."

His "help myself, don't mind if I do" manner frays my edges. Even though I don't remember the plans I had for these things, I did have a plan at one time! And I might remember it and need every last piece of these cribs.

And then—a note?

I didn't think about having to respond to notes.

I don't care what he can do with these things, he can't have them, and I refuse to write back. If I start doing anything on his terms, the whole arrangement will come tumbling down, and if that happens, he'll have to go.

I should get back to those boxes, but I can't. Instead, I forgo the shower and head down to the basement and my studio. Maybe the sight of other supplies will remind me what those cribs were for.

My studio.

I had such lofty hopes for this place, picturing the Eameses or Andy Warhol's The Factory. Maybe calling it a studio has been the problem. Maybe I've thought of myself more highly than I should have in the first place.

I could call it a workshop instead.

But that implies power tools, while I hold my supplies together with wire and twine. The fact that I disassemble them is irrelevant. Of course I'd love to learn to weld; that spot of the blowtorch's blinding light concentrated enough to bond metal seems like the coolest tool an artist can employ, the trump card of artistic processes. But that's some high heat held right there in the palm of my hand. I didn't even trust myself to check my own oil when I had a car. I'd need a class or something to attempt it and even then, I'd be that weird girl who isn't quite as coordinated as the others. "Who's *she*?" they'd whisper behind my back. "And who wears a sweater like that?"

Randi's idea of the arch for the coffee shop doorway comes to mind. I should know how to weld for that. That could be some major incentive right there.

A long worktable attached to the right-hand side of the wall displays my current work in progress. I found a gallon jar of buttons at an estate auction a few years back. Though I didn't think of an immediate project, their beauty was enough, all gathered together behind glass like a tiny display of year-in year-out clothes worn happily, clothes worn out, buttons holding them together in good times and bad, sorrow and joy.

The buttons of choice lay in a spilled swath of brass and

silver, pewter, bone, stone. Plastic amid the more real materials. But not any old plastic, chunky old black plastic buttons that look like somebody carved them out of coal. There are sixteen of these buttons to be precise, large and round, the same size as the lid on a small jelly jar, most likely from a double-breasted, women's overcoat from the fifties or sixties. I can picture it. Pale pink for some reason, and the gloves Miss Fresh 'N' Now bought to go with it? Fabulous and ivory, with a felt beret to match. She bought this coat thinking it would last for years, and it did, as far as construction and quality. But she went just a little too extreme with the style and offered merely an homage to classic couture and not any real commitment to the test of time.

Of course, Miss Fresh felt a little put out. She didn't have the kind of income—or rather, her husband didn't—that allowed for a new overcoat every few years. So when 1968 rolled around, it looked a little dated and made her feel somewhat clownish.

And isn't that just the way?

I separate those buttons and brush the rest aside.

Sixteen buttons.

I hold one up and examine it under the current desk light I've come to favor, lacquered a bright red, the inside of the bell a reflecting white. "Yes, yes," I say. "Let's start with you."

All I can think to do, as I sit there for what feels like hours, is cut off a piece of twine from the ball on one of the shelves at the back of the table and thread it through the nub on the back, knot it, then hang it around my neck.

I turn off the light.

"Well, at least that's something."

Eight

I meet Jack at his rowhouse at three the next day. He's just worked out and is heading toward a shower when I arrive. Smoothie in hand, he offers me one. I'm not stupid. Jack doesn't hold back on his smoothies, and the man loves a good strawberry, my own favorite fruit. So much goes on in that one sweet little package, and no matter how you look at it, how you cut it, it's still pretty.

"Hey, Fi," he says after I take a sip. "I've got a surprise for you. On the bed. Also, I made an appointment for you at Alpha's to get your hair done."

I follow him up the stairs to the floor that's benefited the most from Jack's knack with a hammer, saw, and local contractors. "Why?" I purposely don't follow up with the ringing next question, "What's wrong with my hair?" It's easy to forget Jack's a client sometimes, and I know that's because he wants it that way.

"We're going out."

"I take it this is something more than just the Eastern House."

The Eastern House restaurant in Highlandtown, a Greek diner that seems to check people's licenses to see if they're over fifty, is the least likely place in all of Baltimore for me to be recognized. And their moussaka quite possibly contains all seven keys to happiness, thereby forgoing the need for any kind of self-help guru to pen his thoughts for your progress.

"I know it's against the rules, but, Fia, just this once I need you to do something that's a little out of the ordinary."

"Jack. I don't know."

Our assignation is simple. His place or the Eastern House. If things don't happen at either of these places, they just don't happen. He can't pretend I'm his girlfriend either. This is a business arrangement, pure and simple.

He's been pretty good about this. Until right now, obviously. But I'm going to give him a chance here because Jack's not one to ask for anything without a good reason.

We enter his bedroom. The bed, wide enough for a family of eight to sleep comfortably, sits on a raised platform of mahogany, the mainstay lumber of the room. Everything is clean and straightforward in its design, as if an Asian designer used French influences, decided that cinnamon and a lusty gold were the only two colors in the world, threw in some black, and carefully arranged it all together for "the man who has everything."

Laid out on the bed, a cocktail dress in a retina-vibrating peacock blue provides the first inclination that maybe he's not crazy in asking me to appear in public with him.

"Where did you find this?" I ask.

"New Orleans."

"So what's the occasion?" I roll the chiffon between my fingers. Vintage. And it looks like it will fit perfectly. One of the prettiest dresses I've seen in years.

My hair will definitely have to change if I'm going to wear this.

And hence the appointment.

"Lucy is coming to visit," he says.

He calls his mother by her first name too. Only he does it to her face. She hates it, so he tells me; and he only does it to remind her what a good son he is in all other regards, so he tells me.

"Why is she coming?" Normally he's the one who has to visit her in South Carolina, where he's from.

"Her girlfriends from college are having a weekend in Baltimore together, so she's coming a day early, beginning tonight." He grins and shrugs. "You know, she's got her ways. But Lucy's not bad, all in all."

He's adorable today. I'd probably get tired of him in a typical relationship as he seems to be out of town more than he's home, not to mention the fact that, even at the Eastern House, he warrants all types of feminine attention. The accidental drop. The "Do I know you?" line. They ask for ketchup or Sweet'N Low. Even in the jeans and T-shirts he wears when we go, he can't simply blend in. Plus, he has no clue about any of this. He's a typical engineer in that regard. He thinks the women really do want his Sweet'N Low.

I wouldn't want to be part of all that just because.

Not only that, his world is too regular, even if it does include money, too open and "Here I am!" My world is quirky and dank and littered. Our arrangement is perfect. But still, he's always been kind and sweet to me, so maybe this once I can agree to a departure.

"Just dinner?" I ask, praying the answer is yes.

"No. We're going to a concert too. It's always best to keep Lucy occupied, otherwise she starts prying."

I sit down on the bed. "Is she pressuring you to find a lady? Get married?"

He steps into the dressing room connecting the bedroom to the bath. It's Jack's one little piece of mayhem.

"Yes," he calls as he opens and closes drawers. "I figure a nice dinner and a concert with you along will ease her mind."

"But then she'll start hounding you about our supposed relationship."

He stands in the doorway. "Supposed?"

Sometimes life throws what appears to be a curveball. I want to laugh. Is that what he thinks we've been doing here? Building a relationship?

"Well, you know, we're hardly exclusive."

"Maybe not on every level, but you're the one I can really talk to. You know my secrets."

"I see what you mean."

Sort of. Maybe. In that "I kinda get it in an overarching sense, but the specifics aren't quite adding up" variety of understanding, in that "guestimation" mode. That's fine if you're making lasagna, not so good if you're building a bridge from your head to someone else's heart.

"Okay. I'll go, to dinner only. I can't risk a concert. But as pretty as this dress is, I have a feeling it's more for Lucy than Fia."

"Yeah. You're right."

"I'll find something of my—"

"Take my card and go shopping."

"No. That's way too *Pretty Woman*," I say.

He barks out a laugh. "Yeah, it is. Not sure what I was thinking."

"Honestly. I've got loads of good clothing. Remember?"

"Oh yeah," he says over his shoulder as he steps into the bathroom. "I forget about your other life sometimes."

And this is why I'm here.

I could save a little money and have a good cut and style on Jack's quarter, but the interview is still three months away, and I want it to be fresh and perfect. Having my hair done while sitting in a chair lost its mystique by the time I was fourteen.

"And I'll just do my own hair."

"Suit yourself, Fia. I just want *you* to have a good time and my mother to stop worrying about me."

※

Still in a state of amazement at the sudden turn of events at Jack's, I let myself into the house. The two crib ends lean back against the wall in their original placement, no note attached. In other words—message received all the way to the point that I won't communicate outside of the established boundaries.

First *Pretty Woman*, now *The Jerk*. I seem to be playing the defining roles today.

I don't exactly know what Josia is doing in there, but I know it's an improvement, and I know he won't ask me to pay a cent for it or if he can take some money off of his rent.

I try not to be a taker in this life. I saw enough of that in LA. But I also don't want to be a beggar to another's capacity to give. It's a fine line I don't know how to dance upon, but like any dance, you've got to at least get out on the dance floor and move that first foot a little. Just a tap. Hopefully on the beat.

I scribble a note, *I've changed my mind*, and tape it to one of the crib ends. My heart lightens a bit. Well, good. That feels nice.

It's time to go up to the yellow bedroom and the attached dressing room. It's even larger than Jack's.

Knowing some improvement is happening in one part of the house makes the rest of it feel a little less hopeless somehow.

The marble floor of the entry is still in good shape, as are the handrails and steps leading upstairs. The brass chandelier that most likely welcomed ladies and gentlemen to soirees (whatever they are) and parties, illuminating the fine fabric of their garments and shining its light into their diamonds to throw it back on their healthy necks and bosoms, just needs a good polish to resurrect it.

The ghostly sound of a band leading people in the Charleston fills the hall of my mind, and I'm suddenly thrown into a party scene in *The Great Gatsby*, sitting silent and invisible in the eerie echoes.

It's too much to bear and all too real how people drown themselves in pleasure to dull the pain and the boredom. Just like Daisy in *Gatsby*. I turned my back on the pleasure, but the pain and the boredom remain, and it seems they've piggybacked onto me for good.

I hurry up the steps.

There they all are, "the dresses" on some sort of display, just as they were shortly after I moved in and carefully hung all the expensive designer clothing upon the brass rods. All the shoes are arranged in row after row in the shoe closet. Accessories too.

All a decade out of style.

At least a lot of them. Thankfully, my stylist felt I had a classic rather than siren look and dressed me accordingly: no necklines plunging past my navel in a pathetic attempt to get noticed, no panty-revealing, body-con dresses, no stripper heels with straps. "Your work speaks for you," my best friend, Lila, said. "So you don't need your boobs to keep you in the spotlight."

"Not that I have any," I said.

"Maybe not, but I know where you can get some." And she laughed. Lila was always cracking herself up. I miss her.

But what looked classic ten years ago may not exactly fit the description now. There's always the spin of a trend circling through the design somewhere, and it's too soon to call this stuff vintage. Doubts abound as I look around me at this forsaken space. I only enter it a few times a year, if that.

I should dub this the Hollywood Room, as I had the movers place any box I labeled "miscellaneous" (which was my code word for "my old life") in here. While this room may not be filled floor to ceiling, it's still mindful of a cityscape with its box stacks of uneven heights. The previous owners left all the window treatments behind, and a heavy layer of dust shrouds the palm trees and monkeys on the deep-yellow drapes.

If Oscar is hanging around anywhere, he's here, lying underneath whatever else I threw in these boxes, keeping his rigid form tight like a rocket. I should find him, right? Am I ungrateful or traumatized? I've had a hard time figuring out which it is.

I already know which dress I'm going to pick, so I don't have to stay in here a second longer than necessary. Unfortunately, an open box grabs my attention and I cannot help taking a peek.

A framed snapshot is the first item up for my viewing pleasure, but viewing it brings me no pleasure at all. The capture of myself and Lila reminds me of the day we wore poodle-curly wigs and fat suits, took a cab over to a Golden Corral, and stuffed ourselves with fried chicken, Salisbury steak, mashed potatoes, macaroni and cheese, green beans with ham, salad with creamy blue cheese dressing, Jell-O, pudding, and soft-serve ice cream.

And rolls, rolls, rolls! With butter, butter, butter.

Denying ourselves for the Powers-That-Be just couldn't be maintained a moment longer. She could only do that for so long, she declared in her native Texan accent. However, and though she never said as much, her meal always ended up in the toilet.

We did everything together when we weren't on our respective sets or locations. Lila, a natural blonde with natural boobs, met all the appropriate conditions of the description "hot." She started out on a cable network drama about a family with too many kids, then made a lot of money doing racy teen flicks, showing her breasts and derriere when necessary, kissing a lot of different men, letting them feel her up, and spending a good deal of time on the set in lace bras and undies. I think it tore her up inside. No, I know it did. But in this day and age, nobody told her she was allowed to be bothered. That it was the 2000s, and even though it was just a job and stuff like that didn't bother a lot of people, it was okay if she felt bothered. That it didn't make her a prude, it just made her a private person. And isn't that her right?

Nobody gave her permission to not be permissive. What a screwed-up world we both found ourselves in.

I, on the other hand, tore myself up in heavy dramatic roles, doing my best to research thoroughly the lives of real-world victims and, in a couple of cases, teen psychopaths. Yeah, those were happy films.

Placing the photo back in the box, I shove Lila down deep in my heart where she's been for more years than I knew her in the flesh, close the flaps, then move on. I can't think about her even though she is why I am here now, in Baltimore, in this old house.

But she returns to me in the closet, because the coat she wore on the night she was taken from me is hanging face out from the rack. It is a beautiful coat, wool, light and off-white, but not too off, and stitched with black thread. The buttons were ripped off the night of the incident when someone forced it open to give her air. And though I scrambled around the club, the sticky floors attempting to suck my hands and knees into the grime, I couldn't find even one.

I grab the hanger and turn the coat back to its more sensible position, tucked amid my black wool swing coat and a powder-blue satin capelet I wore to premieres when the weather turned cool in LA.

I lift a pale-beige, almost ivory, sheath down from the rack, as simple as the dot at the end of a sentence. As far as cocktail dresses go, it couldn't be more opposite from the number on Jack's bed.

A pair of simple, low-cut, dark-red pumps, high heels with a rounded toe that I wore to the Golden Globes when I was nineteen, will do just fine. They'll have to. I can't stay in this room a second longer, and I can't quite figure out why I'm here in the first place.

For Jack?

Please.

I'm not sure what kind of woman Jack goes out with for free, but I can almost guarantee she's a lot flashier than this. Still, a bun is a bun and always looks elegant, and I almost never pulled my hair back in the olden days, so there's less chance of being recognized.

It does happen every so often. Thankfully, less and less. And now, the older I get, the more people are unsure they've experienced a "star sighting."

Why the hell people care so much is something I'll never understand. I swear, if given the choice to meet some brilliant yet socially awkward and not-so-good-looking scientist who just gave the world cold fusion and a "Real Housewife from Only the Good Lord Knows Where," a lot of people would go with the housewife.

I hate people sometimes.

Wearing the black swing coat, I emerge from the cab Jack called for me earlier onto Lancaster Street and into Charleston's restaurant. Guess he didn't want to take his mother too far away from South Carolina in tonight's dining experience. I comfort myself that the average online Joe most likely doesn't have a taste for French-inspired Low Country cooking. Judging by my Nutty Bars, I don't either, but I'm willing to give it a try for a man who wants to make his mother happy. And from everything he's ever said to me, she deserves that.

Jack and his mother are already seated in the Palm Room, a dining room rich with dark wood-beamed ceilings, comfortable chairs upholstered in a mild red, and floor-to-ceiling drapes split open to let in the harbor view. White linens, gold-rimmed plates, and simple flower arrangements rest upon the tabletop. In the mirror before me, as large and round as a temple gong, I watch myself walk across the room to their table. An imaginary clapboard slams its black-and-white strips shut.

Scene one, take one.

And there are no other takes, for the record. This is a low-budget film and we don't have much film left, so take that for what it's worth, but no pressure, absolutely no pressure.

Jack stands up and pulls out my chair, then scoops up a set of keys that some woman of indeterminate age due to what looks like a surgeon's knife and an overall game plan to "fight and reduce the signs of aging" has just dropped near his feet.

"Thank you," she says, her blue-tipped lashes dropping against tanned skin.

He awards her a curt yet polite nod of his head.

He gently takes my elbow. "Fiona, I'd like you to meet Lucy."

"Please, call me Mom," says a plain woman in a Sunday church dress with feathered golden hair. Judging by the shade, I'd say she probably did it herself in her very own bathroom and didn't do too bad of a job, actually. Maybe I could have her do mine and save some money for my soon-coming makeover.

Recalling the necessary acting skills, I broadcast a wide grin while remembering I'll most likely never have to see her again and say, "Of course I'll call you Mom if you'd like."

"Now, you, darlin', just sit down right next to me. We girls need to stick together."

Is she for real?

Jack pulls out my chair. "Have a seat, Fi. I already ordered you a cocktail."

"Oooh, thank you! What are you having, Mom?"

Believe me, it feels just as weird to me.

She clasps her hands together, gardener's hands I'm assuming, and rests them in front of her on the table. "Well," she begins, her dripping-with-clarified-butter, coastal Carolina accent coating her words, the softly abraded tones of her voice brought on, Jack told me once, by years of Viceroys and Tareytons. "I normally just sip on a little bourbon, but I let Jack pick for me and I'm trying something new. A gimlet. I've never in my life had a gimlet."

Who even thinks to order a gimlet? I smile at him, the question in my eyes.

He shrugs. "I know my mother, and I know she'll like it."

"And for me?"

"Tonic and lime. What else?"

I laugh. "I guess he knows his women, doesn't he, Mom?" Geez.

"Indeed he does. Now, you just scoot your chair a little closer and tell me all about yourself and why you're willing to put up with a man like Jack. And before you do, let me apologize right here and now for any boorish or unkind behavior on his part. I'll blame them on his father, and maybe his ex-wife too."

Ex-wife?

Jack never mentioned having an ex-wife. But then again, if a woman gets to keep her secrets, so does a man. And he might think he doesn't pay me enough to keep *those* kinds of things to myself. What he doesn't understand is just how much I understand the kind of damage gossip can do.

For the next few hours I play the part beautifully.

❀

Since I'm dressed up, I might as well make the most of it. Jack hired me a cab for the trip home and I feel like I got into a time machine instead. The driver of the old Ford might just have been the coolest man the seventies had to offer. He still wears a fro—not too long, not too short—underneath a leather cap, the kind with a bill and four sections crowned at the top by a button. He's a gentleman cabbie in a chestnut-brown, European-cut leather jacket and crisp, flared dark-denim jeans, opening my door for me and then closing it when I'm tucked in the backseat. His demi boots are polished and his name is Mike.

"They call me Big Mike," he says after sliding into the driver's seat.

Did I mention those clothes were on a six-foot-six frame? And Big Mike must weigh all of one hundred and sixty pounds?

"Tall Mike might have suited you better," I say.

He laughs and the noise fills the cab.

I join in. "Unless they're talking about your big laugh." It's that kind of laugh.

"A man's got to laugh." He turns his head to face me. "You hear what I'm sayin'?"

I nod. "I do. Sometimes there's just not a whole lot to laugh about."

"Now, now, that's just simply not true. You ever heard of Africa? People laugh there all the time, and they ain't got much to laugh about. You know what my mother always said to me?"

"I couldn't say."

"Little Bit, they called her. She was all of five foot tall in nothin' but the feet God gave her, and she had a sad life. Where to, by the way?"

I give him my address.

"Nice. Makes sense with the fancy way you've got about you." He starts the meter and pulls away from the curb.

"Did Jack give you his credit card number?" I ask.

"He sure did. It's all taken care of."

I relax into the old interior. "Did this used to be an Emerald cab, Big Mike?" They were always the nicest cabs, the only company my grandmother would call when she was alive.

"Sure it did! I worked for them for twenty-five years. And then I realized I had a fine clientele all my own. Mrs. Dickson on Mondays for her shopping trip at Mondawmin. The Blake sisters . . . married to each other for the most part, but sweet as the day is long . . . they used me at least three times a week. I always told people," he said in a voice that sounded sage and serious, "don't take a chance. If you need a driver, you just ask for Big Mike, and so they did."

I like him. I like Big Mike. I'm going to ask for Big Mike too. When I can. "Do you have a card?"

He chuckles. "Do I have a card?" Big Mike reaches over as he negotiates a right turn onto Calvert Street and opens his glove compartment. "What's your favorite color?"

"Green. I've always loved green. Then yellow. Then orange. I love daffodils. They're my favorite flower. They have all three colors."

He grasps a stack of business cards held together with the kind of thick blue rubber band that usually hangs out with broccoli. He hands me the stack. "Pick one!"

The cards have been printed on a rainbow assortment of cardstock, just simple black lettering on each with the words:

Don't take a chance. If you need a driver, you just ask for:
Big Mike Reynolds
Get You There Safe and Sound
410-555-1711
Any Time, Any Day, Any Way

I pick the blue. I can't help it. "I know I said I love green, but this is a very pretty blue." I hand him back the stack, then place the card in my evening bag.

"Robin's egg blue," he says, putting the cards back. "My mother's favorite color. So here's what Little Bit always said."

"Little Bit with the big troubles."

"That's it exactly. Hey, you catch on quick!"

I shrug. "What can I say?" I don't tell him that words, having memorized so many of them, now just soak right into me. This talent sounds a lot better than it is. Who wants to remember everything people say to them?

"Little Bit always said to me, 'Mike, if you're not laughing, you're not living.' And people, people are funny things. Never forget that!"

"So that's it? You're telling me to laugh at people?"

All that buildup? I'm a little disappointed.

He laughs. "Not exactly! My, you a funny one. It's just like now, don't you see? What you said? It was funny. People say funny things all the time, but we're so darned serious about it all, we fail to see the humor. Get what I'm sayin'?"

"I'm not sure."

"It's about living here and now, right here in the cab."

"In my own cab? Are you telling me to start driving a cab?" Let's see how funny he really thinks people are.

Apparently quite funny, because Big Mike laughs again. "See? You're catching on."

My acting skills have obviously taken a downturn. But I can't help it. I join in with him, and the goodness I feel soaks through *all* the layers.

We pull up to my house as a text from one of my regulars comes in. By regular, I mean he and I go out maybe twice a year. But Alex is a nice guy. A gamer dude, very lonely.

As he starts to click the meter, I say, "Hold up a sec, Big Mike. Keep the meter running. Can you take me up to Waverly? Jack won't mind. Do you have another scheduled appointment this evening?"

"No, I do not. Where in Waverly?"

"Thirty-Sixth and Frisby."

"Let's go."

And so north we travel, Big Mike chatting it up with me, telling me about his kids. "Do you know I like every single one of them?"

"How many do you have?"

"Four."

"Those are good odds."

He laughs again. I'm starting to see his point. And I listen to him, and to myself, and by the time we pull up to Alex's brick rowhouse with its concrete steps, at least ten of them, leading up a small hill to its small pillared front porch, I realize I don't want this night to end.

This night.

This night I choose not to fool myself that because I only pick nice, lonely guys who will appreciate me in ways the other men won't, I'm not a whore.

"How much do we have on that meter so far?" I ask, hand on the door handle.

"Eighteen seventy-five."

Maybe I should get out. I don't have enough in my purse to keep going. Maybe it's a sign that things aren't going to get any better and I'll be relying on guys like Jack and Mike and that's okay. But a good first step would be not putting one more cent on Jack's meter.

There's only one way out of this. Get out. But just walk home. In my old red heels. Any other way and I'm not standing on my own.

"Is this where you live?" he asks.

"No."

Alex opens the door and waves. Big Mike looks back at me. "I see," he says.

"See what?"

"He your next date? 'Cause here's the thing, miss. You a pretty lady, and you get in the cab paid by one young man, and there's another young man at the other end of the line. Now, it's none of my business, but does the first young man know you used his money to get to the second young man?"

I shake my head.

He stops the meter. "Let's go. Let's get you home."

Big Mike puts the car back in drive, and I feel as if I'm flying, as he seems to forget what happened and we chat some more.

As he pulls up to a curb for the third time that evening, he turns around once again. "You got to live now. Like right now. *Right* now. And you got to decide if your right nows are what you've been hoping for. Are they?"

"Not even close."

"Can you make them that?"

I think about it. All the tools are there, aren't they? Have I just been laying them out like old buttons on a workbench or storing them in boxes and feeling secure about them because at least they're in my own home? "I don't know," I answer. "I don't know if I can anymore."

With terrible timing, Josia pulls up in his big white serviceable, makes-sense-on-every-level truck.

Oh yay! Here's another man that Big Mike gets to see.

"Josia!" he calls as my roommate climbs out. "My man!"

Josia saunters over. "Well, if it isn't my favorite man behind the wheel!"

And they visit like old friends. I don't ask how they know each other, but that they do isn't surprising. I think wise people tend to gravitate toward each other. Maybe wisdom tends to latch onto itself when it finds itself in various places. I don't blame it. There are a lot of fools in this world.

I sigh.

Yep. There certainly are.

Nine

Despite the prior evening's many social interactions, I step with relief into the Bizarre and immediately begin telling Randi about the cribs. She fixes my drink and chatters about her evening spent scouring the Internet in search of someone to fix her espresso machine's wand. To no avail, of course.

I get comfortable at the counter.

While checking my phone, the sugar/caffeine high begins to take hold, and I'm just now realizing how lucky I am that dress still fit last night. I've stayed the same size, okay, but the quality has gone from high-end department store to outlet strip mall. Then again, maybe it's better just to be scrawny than to meet with a really boring trainer three days a week. Because the exciting trainers were even more annoying.

I hated exercising then, and I hate exercising now. But with that interview coming up in a little while, I might want to start getting my arms in better shape.

What am I doing? What if this big interview ends up being something absolutely no one cares about? Bouncing back from that sort of humiliation would be near impossible.

My cell phone rings.

"It's Jessica," I tell Randi.

"Oh, be my guest! This might be good!" She pushes her pencil into her beehive and crosses her arms.

I nod and push the button. "This is early for you, Mother."

"And even earlier out here, Fiona. But I'm sure you remember that."

Of course.

She continues, "Things are really heating up in the tabloids this time. Whoever's writing these things knows what they're doing. And the photos. They are going to some lengths, which makes me feel good about the promotion for the film. Oh, what they can do with a computer now! I look better than ever. Who says these new girls have anything on us?"

Who indeed?

"They even flew your father over to George Clooney's place and snapped pictures of him with that new singer everyone's talking about. Cute girl, but such a *little* girl. What? Twenty-two? And people are lapping it up. He's still on the cutting edge of things, like always, thank God. Have you seen?"

"I don't read the tabloids anymore."

She actually gasps. Not a beefy, "I can't believe you didn't know Aunt Susan used to be Uncle Bob" gasp, but more than an "I think I might have forgotten to turn off the curling iron" intake. "Are you really that disinterested in your father and me?"

All because I don't read the *National Enquirer.*

"Mother—"

"You surprise me, Fiona," she says. I picture her in her "martyr's chamber," an eight-by-eight bedroom that's only packing a single bed and a nightstand, testifying to her vow of never sleeping with any man again in an attempt to make Brandon feel guilty.

Okay. If it worked. But it doesn't.

"But whatever you might think, I almost can't wait to see what happens next!" she says. "And of course people are commenting all over the Internet in my favor. Or so my publicist told me when she called. It's glorious! They think he's such a scoundrel."

I don't tell her this sounds like it all might actually be true and maybe her soon-releasing film is a coincidence. Even if I wanted to say it, she's on a roll.

"They say he's soon to sue me for divorce *and* half my personal fortune! Ha! Even Brandon wouldn't be that stupid. But the public will lap it up!"

"They always do."

"Don't you just love the way the same plot twists work over and over? Brandon is brilliant in some regards. And a complete numbskull in others, granted. But if it keeps us in the news . . . So, Fiona. I'm coming to Baltimore in a few weeks, just to see you."

"Just to see you."

I've been waiting for this call for over ten years, all of my life, actually. Jessica, finally making me a priority. And now that it's here, I can hardly think of anything I'd like less.

"When?"

"In a few weeks, like I just said. But maybe sooner. Should I assume you'll be able to put me up?"

"Hardly. I'm finally renovating around here. You'll have to get a hotel room."

"Well, if that suits you best." She seems relieved, though. "I'll leave it to you to find something suitable. And while I'm in Baltimore, I want to visit the offices of Jasper Venn and his studio as well. I've always wanted to guest star in a gritty police drama, and my agent thinks that now's the time."

"Actually, that sounds like fun." Big Mike could drive us. There most likely would be no pictures taken. Add to the fact that gritty police dramas have dwindled under the hot stream of meth and motorcycle clubs, zombies, and three-martini lunches, and there's no reason why I shouldn't take a stroll around Jasper's corpse of a set. Shoot, maybe Jessica's presence would make the show itself a zombie of sorts, resurrected but still saying things like, "I am a gritty cop with a sad past and addiction or religion issues. Uuuuuhn."

She pauses. "I wouldn't want to bother you with it."

"The show is a little old-fashioned," I say, wincing at my own childish reaction to her. Once again, rejection.

"It is?"

"Well, kinda. The show is on its last legs, if you want the truth."

She says nothing, then, "What about other shows? What are the biggies, then?"

"None that film in Baltimore."

"Hmm." I hear her tap the phone with her fingernail. Will she come see me anyway?

"Are you sure you want to come now? I mean, with the renovations and all?" I ask above the noise of the woodpecker inside my phone.

She stops tapping. "Nonsense. I've never seen your home. It's about time for that, Fiona. You've done the hermit thing just a little too long now."

No. I haven't.

"Well, let me at least think about it."

"Think all you want, I'll still be booking that flight. I wish you didn't live across the country. You know I'd much rather take the train."

After we ring off, I watch Randi and sip on my latte. That woman right there with her sweet little shop and her nice customers? She has the life.

❀

The golden evening arrives accompanied by a pink that's more ballet slipper than cotton candy. I don't feel like going on a date, and I don't usually work in my studio at night because the basement transforms into a mad murderer's workshop, the foul old lair of one who employs odd devices to ply his trade and sneaks into my basement to do it. And that's enough said about that! I always refused to do horror flicks for a reason.

I should try to at least think about what I'm going to do for the Bizarre. But all the supplies down there don't help in this regard, okay. The dog-eared vision of a box of doll parts has not gone unrealized. But the accompanying idea was to make a work decidedly un-creepy with them. It's a tall order, and no idea, shimmery and bright with promise, has entered my mind yet. One doll in particular continues to fascinate me, though, a little boy doll dressed in a velvet short-pants suit and a white shirt with a lace collar designed to swallow his head if the situation warrants it. He should look like he'll end up in heels and a wig someday, but there's something defiant in his eyes, as if he's saying, "Oh, don't you worry about me, lady. I've planned quite the revenge for having to wear this outfit. Just wait until I turn fifteen." Maybe I should just pull him out and pitch the rest.

It's just the impetus I need.

I trek down to that dark basement, yank the gray string hanging like a weary subway commuter from the light fixture, and go right for the box. I tuck Edwin, for that is what he looks like, under my arm, then haul the box up the inside steps and out to the back porch to join the other boxes.

According to Big Mike, there's hope in the present moment,

and presently I actually feel like going through the boxes I stacked out here just before Josia moved in. If I don't make the most of it, I'm an idiot. And I take a minute to talk myself out of talking myself out of it like I always seem to do.

I really am my own worst enemy.

The large moon shines in sympathy tonight, providing enough clear light to complete the task. By the time eleven rolls around, I've separated the items into a keep stack and a discard stack. Edwin sits on the iron chaise wondering what I'm going to do with him now, and truthfully, I just don't know. But I simply will not leave him here on the porch. He'll have to come inside with me. This horrid doll outfit that smells exactly like the basement has to go, and right now.

Here's to nothing being better than something.

So I strip Edwin bare immediately and pitch his ridiculous velvet suit with the giant lace collar onto the discard pile. Passing through the hallway, no light beams from under Josia's door. I don't think he's come home yet and now it's almost eleven fifteen. I hope he's okay. But the crib ends had gone missing again when I woke up earlier in the day, so I know he's continuing his work. I picture a forge fire escaping its confines and burning down the whole operation.

That would be so sad. Maybe I'll get to see the forge someday. I don't know. Extending me an invitation at this point would be way out of line, and Josia knows that.

I pour a glass of chocolate milk, then grab my phone on my

way upstairs. I bathe poor naked Edwin in my bathroom sink, scrubbing years of grime off the porcelain. In my bedroom I dress him in one of my old white T-shirts, the smallest one I can find. He looks like a little ghost.

Ten

The next morning I practically collide with Josia as I navigate the last step and spin toward the corridor. The "delightfully delicious, slow-roasted flavor" of my instant coffee must have been calling to me more loudly than I thought.

"Oh!" I veer to the right. "Sorry!"

Laughter emits from behind a stack of boxes in his arms. "Hang on and let me get these in the truck. I need to show you something if you've got the time."

Somebody stop me from laughing. I've got nothing but time.

"Wait!" I cry. "Are those the boxes from the porch?"

"Yes." He stops and turns around. "I figured these were part of a pile you were wanting to throw out." A doll arm flops over the top box. "But if you don't want me to haul them away, just say the word."

This is it. I stand upon the border of the land of no excuses. He's willing to get this stuff out of here. Gone. Everything I don't want. I don't have to figure out if there's a junk man who hauls stuff away, if I have to rent a truck to take unwanted items to Goodwill, or if I could just put them on the street and let nature take its course. This is a hard thing to figure out.

I'll bet Jack's mom doesn't have a house full of supplies like I do. I bet she enjoys a cup of tea in peace every morning. I know Jack does. And Big Mike? Well, he's got the things he loves, and there are probably a lot of those because he seems to have a lot of love, but I'm sure he drives by garage sales and junk on the side of the road all the time and never stops to load up the trunk.

"I'd be grateful if you would."

"Good. Be right back."

I watch him from the long, slender window to the right of the door as he walks down the front path, the same spring to his step as always, and sets the boxes in the back of his pickup.

"Let me help," I say when he enters the house.

"How about making me a cup of coffee while I finish carting out the rest?"

Before I can really think about all the major implications of this, I agree.

He stands at the doorway to the kitchen five minutes later. "I've got something to show you," he says. "Shouldn't take but a minute."

"Okay." I don't have it in me to tell him he's breaking one of the rules. The man is, after all, hauling away my follies. "Coffee's almost done."

I don't invite him into the kitchen. No sense in going crazy with the latitude I'm extending this morning.

✺

Water now boiling in the pot, I pour it into two mugs, one a dollar-store burgundy, the other a dollar-store green, where I've already spooned in the space-age coffee *crystals*— because they're so much more *essential* than the humble old coffee bean.

For a brief moment, my grandfather's face comes to mind, how at the end of each meal he'd have a Sanka. "Here's to some things being better than nothing," he'd always say, raising his coffee cup, a pink plastic one that matched my grandma's everyday plates. I moved here to Baltimore to be close to him and now he's out at College Manor, unable to guide a spoon to his mouth.

"Here's to some things being better than nothing." I raise my mug to Josia.

He raises his, and we sip simultaneously in that tentative, inaugural, "I'm-not-sure-how-hot-this-really-is" sip.

Josia wants to wince, I can tell, and not from the temperature. I guess not everyone appreciates space-age crystals the way I do. "You ready?" he asks, curving the index and middle fingers of his left hand around the curlicue handle of the mug.

They're beautiful hands. Not in the perfectly groomed

manner of the manicured men of this world. They're large, but so graceful I can imagine my own placed in one of his as he helps me aboard a sailboat. And I'd trust him not to falter. They're the hands of a man who knows what he's doing, who knows what needs to be done and exactly the time to move forward.

Timing is everything. If Hollywood teaches you nothing else, it's that.

Josia's right hand circles around the doorknob of cut glass at his bedroom door, twists to the left, and pushes inward.

"Just one second," he says, slipping inside. But before the door closes behind him, I catch a glimpse of the room in a quick flash of red walls and gleaming floors.

How about that? I muse. For some reason it doesn't feel wrong to want to rely on him like it does other men. But maybe it isn't about reliance. Maybe he just makes a fine teacher, and his way is a way to emulate.

He backs out a few seconds later, an iron piece about the size of a small dinner plate in one hand, the cursed coffee still in the other.

"For the porch," he says, handing me a sun, somehow delicately rendered, its features pierced into the metal surrounding it. "I made it for you."

"This will look so pretty hanging from the ceiling. Thank you!"

He shuts the door. "Good! I'm glad you like it." He takes another sip, then downs the rest of the coffee in a few what must be throat-scalding swallows. Then again, the man does work around intense heat. He probably breathes in air every day that would char my throat. "I've got to get to the forge. Maybe we'll bump into each other again."

And in that last sentence, all my fears are assuaged.

After he's gone and I'm finished with my coffee, having sipped it on my now-cleared porch, I hang the sun, and it makes me happy that someone made something just for me.

❈

Maybe Josia's inspiration will continue dripping off onto me. I head down to my workshop, take off the button necklace, and stare at the table before me, wondering what to do next. I decide to string all the buttons onto their own length of twine.

Why buttons?

I don't know. But these hold a sort of fascination for me. And I think about my maybe-project at the Bizarre and hope and pray that something right here will inspire me.

After the stringing is done, I arrange them all in lines, knotted string beginning at the top, leading down to the button.

I watch them.

"Tell me what to do with you," I ask, or maybe demand. "I need you to tell me what to do."

❈

So I can't stand it anymore. After enduring a chilly bike ride and eating Subway takeout on the back porch, and wishing for more creative inspiration the likes of which you see in documentaries of artists obsessed, I wad up my sandwich wrapper and pitch it in kitchen garbage can number three.

Thoughts of those red walls in Josia's room have plagued me all day. The floors too. And that quick flash of a visual can only lead me to believe that's the least of it.

He said to knock anytime, okay, and right now fits that description, so I step across the hall to his doorway and rap five times.

Nothing. Of course. He's gone. His truck is gone and he most likely will come home after I've gone out for this evening's date. I've been thinking a lot about my escorting life since the ride with Big Mike. But tonight I'm going over to Jack's, thank goodness.

I knock again. Wait.

What's that I hear? Surely I'm not imagining that muffled, "Come in," am I?

I push the door open and step inside. Room empty. Guess I did imagine it. But as long as I'm here, and this is the present moment and all, well, wouldn't you go in?

✳

What I'm not imagining is this room. The sneak preview provided earlier, while beautiful, did nothing to prepare me for a full production beyond my own imagination.

The red walls are a darker, softer shade that invites the eyes, a shade more Christmas than Valentine's, a shade that conjures up family dinners, not heart-shaped beds in the Poconos.

And the woodwork gleams like the floors. The missing and injured portions have been carefully replicated and replaced, stained in a mahogany shade and protected by a glossy coat that picks up the light descending in diamond shapes from the repaired window.

So the woodworking required power tools, obviously, but why is there no smell? Paint? Stain? Polyurethane? That's even more of a mystery.

A black platform bed rests in the spot his cot occupied, a single mattress covering the top, a white down comforter topping that. A single pillow, plumped and smooth, crowns it all. All that softness looks as if it would suck every care I own from every cell in my body. It is the very picture of the utterance, "Ahhh."

Josia replaced the card table with a two-by-four piece of birch plywood, finished to match the woodwork, and attached to the wall with hinges. Four twelve-by-twelve-inch matching boxes beneath hold his clothing.

Over the bed, a shelf supports his books. I take a look. All of them are design books, except for a few on auto repair. Two stand out from the rest, obviously read for years: *The Art of War* and *The Art of Peace*.

A floor lamp he rescued from the back porch has been painted a wrought-iron black; its shade, fashioned from four storybooks, stands in the corner near the bathroom door.

Even knowing the man as little as I do, I'm certain he didn't reserve his improvements just for this room. The bathroom might just be a cave of wonders, and since I'm trespassing in here already, I might as well go ahead and take a peek.

Again, my imagination did it no justice.

Not surprisingly, his magic has infiltrated this room as well. Does the man ever sleep?

While I was out in the night on my empty romps, he was in here, replacing the tile floor with the slate stacked in the yard and using the leftover octagonal floor tiles to patch the gaps in the wall. Only he didn't just fill in the missing rectangles, but created a sunburst pattern starting in the upper corner of the wall by the bathtub, the tub he must have lacquered over because it practically glows, a clean so clean it promises nothing but a very peaceful bath devoid of those questions we ask ourselves:

Who has been in this tub before me?

What kinds of germs are somehow surviving in the pores and pocks of this thing?

Will I get some kind of venereal disease here that, if forced to explain, nobody will believe came from simply taking a bath?

Am I gross because I like baths more than showers?

Even more wonderful are the crib ends, and how glad I am he used them, one with a mirror mounted to it and placed over the pedestal sink, another for the front of a new cabinet placed against the opposite wall.

I can't help but chuckle at what he's done with the light

fixture over the mirror. He painted the fixture itself black, but now, instead of the grimy globe, the bubble from a child's push-able "popcorn popper" diffuses the light around the room, livening it up further.

Red towels hang from two wrought-iron bars. Clearly made in his forge, they're mounted on the walls, a small one by the sink and a longer one by the tub. At each end a little robin figurine sings.

Beautiful. Just beautiful.

Maybe in my haste to draw up the rules, I should have thought them through a little more, but upon further inspection of Josia's room, it's evident the old coffeemaker and microwave simply don't belong in here. I've never once smelled the aroma of coffee or food emanating from his room. He just put them here to be nice.

Is that the person I've become, the person for whom people do things they really don't want to do? That difficult aunt you always tuck a little gift in your bag for so you don't have to hear her criticize you? That blunt guy friend you can't really tell anything to because you're afraid of his reaction?

So I scribble out a note.

Use the kitchen from now on and feel free to do whatever you'd like in there,

mister nice guy, because if you've got all this in you, I want more.

But just the kitchen.

I add to be clear about it. Everybody should be able to use a kitchen if there's one nearby. What kind of person rents out a room and doesn't allow the renter to use the kitchen?

Me?

I tape it to his door and then write a PS upon further thought.

If you want to get rid of the rest of the crib ends, or use the wood however you see fit, please do so.

Eleven

Sitting once again on the outer wall of Fort McHenry, I muse on the mystery of Josia. No young lovers with nothing better to do enhance the scene before me today, but that's just as well. I want to clear my mind, not observe the tender workings of the world, tenderness the world seems to lack. Or maybe my growing years—years on sets, in makeup chairs, at parties and photo shoots; years of having to fly hours at times to whichever parent felt the most guilty for being gone; years being awakened at 5:30 a.m., if I was lucky, by Elena our housekeeper; years of questioning the sincerity of every friend I ever made and "boyfriend" I ever had—colored my vision, somehow taking away the ability to notice those tender moments unless they're playing like a Hallmark movie right before me like those two young lovers by the waters of a glistening river.

A chill wind ruffles the water today, my beast of a sweater unable to cut it much. It's been so long since I talked to Brandon.

And as much satisfaction as giving him a title other than sperm donor would provide, I simply cannot do otherwise. I miss my father.

He wasn't all bad.

Am I insane?

Before I can talk myself out of it, I dial his number. (Before too much credit is given, I should disclose that it always goes straight to voice mail.)

"Hello there, Fia!"

Figures, doesn't it?

"Hi, Brandon. Just calling to find out how much of the latest tabloid exploits are based on a true story." I try to sound as sour as possible.

"Thirty-three and one-third percent. The woman is not true, that I'm filing for divorce is true—"

"Does Mom know that?"

"She should. The papers were delivered three weeks ago."

Oh. "So what else isn't true?"

"I'm not trying to get into her bank accounts."

Well, phew. I'm glad he's got that much to him. Figures Jessica zeroed in on that. Of course, she didn't dream I'd actually call him. That only happens once a year, if even.

"Is this time for real?" I ask, a little shocked at the harshness of my tone.

Unsaid: because you've jerked her around like this for the last thirty-five years.

He clears his throat, a no-no for someone who uses his voice to make a living, but he's never been able to give up the habit. Like his girlfriends. "Last time I checked, Fia, you legally gave up any right to ask me questions like that."

I hang up. So be it.

And I'm whisked up in the grip of my own memory, set back down on the set of *Dog Ears*, the only television series I ever did, a one-season-only experiment by Gregory Campbell, a famous producer/director of epically funded motion pictures. It was some of the best work I ever did, not just up to that point, but forever and ever. Since my future in acting seems doubtful, I guess I'll dare to admit, *Dog Ears* is the best work I will ever do.

I was only twelve.

To this day, it has a cult following. No network, cable or otherwise, was willing to pay the price for Campbell's genius, so *Dog Ears* went to video after pirated copies sailed out like ships spreading the plague. Campbell was smart enough to get control back and sold enough VHSs to probably pay off the mortgage on his ski lodge in Aspen.

I paid the price, though. The kicker is, he comes off as such a nice guy to 99.9 percent of the world. It would be like accusing the father on *7th Heaven* of such behavior. Who in the world is going to believe Reverend Eric Camden is capable of such things?

"Couldn't you have seen it was more than either/or?" I ask them out loud over the waters, my voice captured and muffled by the heaviness of the wind.

All these years later I can see the obvious solution: pull me out of the business and keep up with your precious work. Elena and I would have been just fine there in the hills, swimming, carpooling, shopping for school shoes . . . although hanging out at a school with a group of friends feels as foreign as going to live in remote Tibet. Even Elena, just Elena, would have been enough, though.

My phone chimes and a text message from Jack lights up the screen. *I'm free. Got a couple of hours? Come on over if you can.*

Might as well.

❋

After a soak in the hot tub on Jack's back deck, the mellow temps of a warm spring allow us to lounge in ivory bathrobes and sip on beers he bought from a local brewery. A pair of his giant tube socks swaddle what would have been my cold feet, despite the mellow air around us.

"What did you think of Lucy?" he asks.

"*Mom* was great. I didn't realize you came from such a normal upbringing."

"Fi, everything seems normal to you when compared to your own childhood." He raises his beer to me, looking like everything every woman would want. So why does he call me to come over? A man who looks like Jack shouldn't be paying for female companionship.

"Then how about this? She seemed really down-to-earth."

"That's Lucy. But normal? No way." He swigs.

Lucy owns an ice-cream truck and is an avid gardener; she works like a wind-up clock for three months until the summertime winds die down and the small feet that ran over hot asphalt are tucked safely back in their school shoes. She spends the next nine months in either her yard or greenhouse, designing the flowers for small weddings and arrangements for all seven of the churches in her town each Sunday.

So Randi's got the life at her Bizarre, and Lucy most definitely has the life down there in South Carolina. What is their secret? How did they decide just to do stuff with their day?

Jack sets the bottle on his knee. "Well, she loved you, Fia. Saw beyond the act, not surprisingly."

Like mother, like son.

We sit awhile longer in silence until the evening sky takes over the afternoon, then chitchat the way we are able to do (I love that about him) until I can't stand it any longer.

"How do you view me, Jack? I mean, the other day . . ."

"I went out on a limb."

"I'm trying to understand here. What do you think has been going on between us all these years?"

He sets down his bottle on the tray between us, looking leading-man sexy without the leading-man arrogance.

He sits up, swings his feet around, plants them at the side of his chair, and leans toward me. "What's been going on with me and what you *think* has been going on with me have been two different things. I am fully aware of what the nature of this relationship has been to you so far, Fia. But what you've seen as payment has been anything but from my viewpoint."

I raise a hand. "Hold up a sec. You mean you've been going along with the arrangement, but not really."

"Not as far as I'm concerned. As far as you're concerned, by the letter of the law."

"But why?"

He reaches out and places his fingertips along the side of my face. I grab them, squeeze them together, and remove them. But I keep hold, our hands landing together in my lap.

He closes his blue eyes against the orange of the sun, opens them again, and looks into mine. It isn't forthrightness or courage I see there, just the windows to an open heart. "I've loved you since I was thirteen years old and saw you in *Everyone Lives*. I bought the Most Beautiful People edition of *People* when you were in it. I defended you to everyone during your various falls and exploits, and when I saw you three years ago, I knew I would take whatever you had to offer and give whatever I could."

Unconditional love? Well, I don't believe in it, not surprisingly. But this is probably the closest I'll ever come to receiving it. "But you've played the role so perfectly."

"Yes."

My heart feels as if rain is pelting it from the inside out.

"I'd better go." Get the hell out of here, I mean.

He sighs, releases my hands, and stands. "I knew you'd say that."

"I can see my way out."

Of course I can. I'm very good at that.

Twelve

After my departure from Jack, I began having tea with Josia after he arrived home some evenings, sometimes saying little, sometimes chatting about the trivialities of our day, but never anything deep or profound. It's as if he knows I've allowed my thoughts to consume me so thoroughly these past ten years, I don't want to talk about them anymore.

On a rainy night in May, sitting cross-legged on his bed across from where I sit on his desk chair, he confesses he is itching for another project.

"What about the kitchen?" I ask. "I mean, since you're allowed there anyway."

His eyebrows rise. "The kitchen. Really? Good. Yes, I think I can come up with something you'll like."

"What about welding?" I ask.

"Yes?" he asks, reaching for the remainder of the Nutty Bar he started at the beginning of our teatime.

"Do you know how to do it?"

"Yes. It's quite a satisfying experience gluing materials together that don't seem like they should be glued."

I laugh. "Yes! That's it."

"Why do you ask?"

I tell him about Randi's suggestion for the entry arch to the Bizarre.

"Oh yes. That sounds good. Very good."

"So I think I'll take a new tack on clearing things out. Keep the things you need a blowtorch to glue together."

He raises his mug. "I like it." Then takes a sip.

I want him to offer to help me learn but realize the fences I erected in our relationship prohibit him from doing so.

Drat. And I thought I was being so smart.

I'll ask later, though. Since the rift with Jack, I just haven't been in the mood to change things, and that interview is coming up sooner rather than later. I've been walking more to get in shape, but how much difference is it really going to make?

So far, for the trip to New York for the interview, I've got a thousand dollars saved. I want to stay at the St. Regis because that trumps all other hotels there, as far as I'm concerned. And I'll need to arrive in a limousine in a fabulous designer outfit because this isn't just about the interview; this is about playing a role from the moment my high heels descend in the city to the second they leave. I have to be fabulous on the interview set as well—which is yet another outfit—and I have to be convincing. It's the only way to trump Jessica's book.

I figure another three thousand dollars and I should be set. I wish Lila were here. She'd walk me through it all. And she'd make it fun.

❈

After our tea is finished I head upstairs and clear the clothes off of my bed, trying as best as I can to put them away. I whisk up the dress I wore to dinner with Jack's mom, along with the red high heels, and head into the Hollywood Room. And there it still is, Lila's coat, hanging in the closet.

I throw down the clothing and rush over.

The sudden freshet of grief scours off the scab long covering past pains, revealing how sharp it all still is. I reach out and run my fingertips down the beautiful ivory coat she once owned, the coat the EMTs pulled off of her body, yanking it open to expose her chest. Have you ever seen an overdose?

I truly hope you haven't.

Wrapping it around me, I hug the fabric, hold the collar up to my nose, and breathe in deeply. *Please*, I ask the soft, brushed wool. But her aroma is gone. Ten years is such a long time.

Lila's coat still around me, I'm standing in front of my worktable looking at my button strings arranged in two lines of eight buttons each. This is the best arrangement yet.

In fact, this is *the* arrangement.

Right?

Now, what it will be arranged upon or with, I don't know, but I'm pretty sure a blowtorch will be unnecessary.

I place my hands on my hips and twist my waist as my eyes scan the front of the stacks of boxes and supplies.

Yes, they should definitely be mounted to something, okay. I remember those remaining crib ends, but shush the idea because for some reason my brain has moved on from the baby idea, and like a woman who wasn't all that keen on having children finding out she's barren, I realize it's no big deal.

Well, the mounting surface will reveal itself. With all these things around me, how can it help but do so? I'll just have to remind myself to keep my eyes open and looking around because you never know when something unexpected will come your way.

Hopefully that's a good thing.

I take off the coat and drape it over the back of my work stool. Maybe Lila, in her own way, will lend a little inspiration.

Randi swirls a cleaning rag, shaking her head. "Wow, that's a lot of work he's doing. And for free?" She squints, her mouth dropping into a grimace.

"What do you mean?"

She shrugs.

My shoulders mimic hers, but with less skepticism and some apology for my apparent naïveté adjusting the slant a tad. "I think he's just a workaholic, but doing it in a completely lovable way."

Randi places her hand on her hip, the rag flowing back over her curled fingers like the bustle on a lady's ball gown. "To be honest, Fiona, I think it's a little odd. Who does that sort of thing for someone? I mean, he's got to know he's not going to live there forever, you know?"

"Maybe he's just a nice person, Randi."

She laughs. "Maybe I'm too jaded for my own good." Then she finishes up the counter, shining it with a towel in broad strokes from the front edge to the back.

My phone rings and the word *Brandon* lights up the screen.

"My dad," I whisper. "That's odd."

"Take it away!" Randi says, grinning at the prospect of listening in.

"Hi, Brandon."

"Fia, hi. I'm coming to Baltimore for a benefit luncheon for Center Stage."

"So why are you calling me, then?"

"I need your help, Fia."

I want to bark out a snotty little laugh, but the truth is, he's never asked for my help before.

"What is it?"

"Would you come with me to the benefit, not tomorrow afternoon but the next? Center Stage is where I got my start. It would mean more to me than I could say if you accompanied me."

"Okay."

A moment of, I presume, stunned silence ensues and he says, "Well, great. Are you sure? You know a photographer is likely to snap us together."

I hadn't thought of that, but even if I had, I'd like to think I would have made the right decision and say, "That's okay too."

Talk about something unexpected coming your way. I didn't mean this. I didn't mean a family loyalty scenario at all. I meant winning the lottery, or helping someone on the street and finding out he was a monk from Tibet with the wisdom of the ages tucked inside and sent on a mission to teach the first person who helped him in America the secret to peace and happiness, and you're the lucky winner, Fiona Hume.

Something like that. Not the father I divorced sixteen years ago.

"All right, Fia, thank you. I'm going to hang up before you can change your mind. I'll call you when I land tomorrow evening. Plane gets in at 7:35 p.m. but I'll be renting a car. And thank you again."

True to his promise, the line goes dead before I can say even a quick good-bye.

"Well, way to go, Fiona," I say to the phone, then proceed to relate the conversation to Randi.

"Really? You're going to appear in public with Brandon Hume? I really will have to see it to believe it."

"Oh, you'll see it. You can believe that completely."

She stifles a laugh with her hand. "Is he anything like his character in *Galaxy Goons*?" she asks, then, "Hold up," as she attends to a customer just approaching the counter, a younger man wearing skinny jeans even goofier than *Galaxy Goons*.

Galaxy Goons. The goofball comedy came out when I was fifteen. Everyone called my father a fool for starring in what turned into a summer blockbuster and an immediate, quotable classic all at the same time. "When *Airplane!* collides with *Spaceballs* and *Heathers, Galaxy Goons* is the result," one prominent reviewer said, and he was right.

It's Brandon's one comedic standout, a hilariously shining departure in an otherwise serious career, and he's taken it pleasantly in stride. "Here's to something being better than nothing!" he said in his interview on *Good Morning America*.

"No," I say. "He's a little smarter than Captain Quirk."

"Are you putting him up at your place?" she asks.

"Oh, sure. Yes. I'll just kick Josia out of his room."

"I'm sure that would go over big."

My heart begins to pound, thinking of seeing my father again. "The sad thing is, Josia probably wouldn't mind."

Merely the thought of that gentle man slows the pace of my anxious heart.

Thirteen

Brandon is due to arrive in less than twenty-four hours, and Josia is working late tonight on a set of outer doors for a chichi new restaurant in Prince George's County.

I was really looking forward to the nightly cup of tea, having worked so hard in the garden earlier—some weeds, stalky and woody, required more exertion than I prefer. Pulling with my back, my legs, my stomach—now that's what a workout should be. The Farm Workout. I could make a million getting rich people to work a farm, the produce of which I could sell for profit. What an idea!

Josia, had he been around, would have appreciated my efforts, and he would have listened to me dream a little about what that newly cleared patch of ground might become with a little forethought, love, and time.

The earth smelled so good. Clean and new and yet so ancient at the same time. How can that even be?

I wanted to tell Josia about it. And even more so, I wanted to tell him about my father. He would have some good advice. He would probably tell me to be open and honest with Brandon because that's Josia's way. But I won't let my father think I've frittered away my earnings when part of my reason for filing was the supposed mismanagement on the part of my parents' financial manager. Yes, Brandon, I did a bang-up job on my own, as you can see by my crumbling yet genteel home and my daily trips to Subway.

No, thanks. I don't want to touch the money I've saved for the New Big Reveal. I'll have to take care of some things on my own. Take a little sashay down to the pharmacy and buy a little something to perk up my hair.

So I call Jack because he can give Josia a run for his money when it comes to calming down a case of the nerves. I've never initiated us getting together, and apparently that was the right instinct. When his phone goes to voice mail after only the second ring, sadness envelops me. Why did he have to confess the way he felt? That ruins everything.

That he chose to love me when I gave him no reason to think our arrangement was anything other than business doesn't make me feel any better for having, what amounts to, broken his heart.

In any case, none of the men in my life are available right now.

I wonder if Big Mike makes house calls.

❋

A composition book in my lap and a glass of chocolate milk beside me, I sit outside in the backyard, ready to tackle another flower bed. But first—a plan. A visit from Brandon is huge. Until now, I've always remained firm about parental visits. This feels different, though. I write at the top of a sheet in bold letters:

How to Look Like You're Doing Well Financially on a Shoestring When You Aren't, by Fia Hume

Okay.

1. Drag out the expensive clothing.
2. Act confident.
3. By all means do whatever you must do to keep your father away from your dilapidated and obviously neglected city mansion that eats away your money day by day.
4. Lip gloss, lip gloss, lip gloss.

He'll expect to come over right after he lands, so I'll thwart that by meeting him at his hotel for a late dinner, and then the benefit luncheon the next day, and hopefully that will just be that and back to Idaho with you, padre! It's not like he was asking me to hang with him the entire time he's in town.

But for now, the garden calls me back.

A brick wall surrounds the rectangular garden, square stone posts breaking up the space every twelve feet, those closest to the porch supporting pineapple finials.

A week ago I started removing the dead cherry tree in the middle by sawing off branches, and now it stands, a trunk with its upper, vertical branches pointing skyward like a drummer's snare brush. It will just have to stay that way for the present.

Today I'm determining which shrubs to save and which to keep. Someone loved azaleas, that much can be determined, and as the blooms are now fading and wilting around the edges, I can still decide which colors to keep. I'm going with the bright pink and the red.

I finish my milk and enter the outside door of the basement, crawl over the last year or two's worth of supplies toward the spot where some old rakes and shovels lean up against a side wall. I grab a shovel and, stepping over a box of gears from some mysterious machine, a tine from a rusted rake digs its jagged finger through my pajama bottoms and down the flesh of my outer thigh.

I drop the shovel immediately, my right hand grabbing the offending implement and pushing it away as the fire of jagged pain flows down the wound and blood begins to flow.

Gush, actually.

The quickness of the crimson flow shocks me as much as the handle of the rake as it bounces against the hot water heater, sending it back in my direction. Thankfully, my left hand, now streaked in blood, springs up to block my face.

A rusted rake! Why did it have to be rusted? But then, how could it not be? Everything about my life has oxidized.

I scramble slowly over the basement's junk offerings, doing my best to hold my thigh and stanch the flow at the same time. Never has all this stuff looked so worthless. And not just worthless, but decidedly a deficit. Worse than worthless. In my way. In my way. It's all in my way.

I stumble over boxes and around at least fifteen straight-back chairs. Then coatracks, a couple of steel desks, and more boxes. Boxes and boxes. There's even a box of boxes.

Somebody please get me out of here!

Finally, I hobble up the basement steps until, in the kitchen, having left heavy drops of scarlet in a line down the hallway, I run cold water and nab the roll of paper towels on the counter. I begin to dab at the gash. But despite my flimsy attempt at first aid, the blood continues to soak through the paper towels at a rate that frightens me. It's going to need stitches. Hopefully before a transfusion is necessary.

There's nobody else to call but Jack. This time, when his voice mail picks up, I leave a message.

"Jack, I know you're probably off in Dubai or Tahiti or Alaska or something, and I know you're upset and want nothing to do with me anymore, but I need your help. I just had a stupid run-in with a rusty rake. I need stitches I think, and I don't want to ride my bike over to the emergency room. So if you could call me back if you get this right away, I'd appreciate it. Thanks. I'm sorry."

I end the call and suddenly the bright idea to call a cab lights up the darkness of "I'm-thirty-two-years-old-and-clueless," and I can only hope the sight of my own blood veiled the obvious solution to my problem because right now I feel more stupid than that rake.

And there it sits, Big Mike's card, where I left it by the coffee-maker on kitchen table number one. Every once in a while my cluttered ways help me out.

Don't take a chance, the card says. *Any time, any day, any way.*

"I'm ten minutes away," he says after I've spilled out the story. "Can you hang on?"

"I'll be out front."

"Hang in there, baby. Hang tight."

I love him.

I love Big Mike.

In the ten minutes it takes for him to arrive, I bind a towel around my thigh, relieved the pressure is working to keep the wound from soaking the terrycloth completely. I tape it in place with duct tape from a roll I keep atop kitchen table number two. Before I can hurry upstairs to put on a decent skirt or dress, Big Mike arrives, honking furiously. He jumps out and runs up the walk.

Wait till he gets an eyeful of me in dusty-pink pajama bottoms with a bloody tear at the left leg, my beastly black sweater, and, jamming my feet inside them, a pair of green Wellingtons so old the rubber has begun to dry rot.

Beautiful.

❋

"University okay?" he asks, helping me into the backseat of his clean cab.

"Okay. Whatever you think."

He slides into his seat. "Folks seem to have the best response when I pick them up there." He pulls out with that cabdriver ease, that slouchy curve, quick yet smooth, and the picture of steady nonchalance. "I do this all day every day," it says. I need that kind of calm right now.

He heads up Howard toward Green Street and a hospital so large my stitches will seem like a breather compared to all the victims carted in by Medevac.

Big Mike turns off the talk-radio heads on WBAL and the local diatribe against our mayor and the governor. Politics. Even messier than my basement. Brandon always says when asked about politics in interviews, "A sector of society that's even more in need of a good spanking than Hollywood."

I have to stifle a laugh. *Maxim* first recorded the quote and I don't think a single American citizen disagreed.

"Let me put on some soothing music," Big Mike says, switching to FM and a classical station.

What am I going to do? This will eat up the rest of my afternoon and I'll have no time to get ready for Brandon's arrival. I may not have a stylist anymore, but I remember how to present myself as a star. Still, I need a good three to four hours to do it. So much of it is about the hair.

After gardening, I planned to head over to Rite Aid, purchase a color rinse and some hot rollers because, in all my supply purchases, I never brought home beauty equipment. I wanted to stay as far away from artifice as possible.

And hair spray. Gotta have hair spray.

But now I'll be lucky if I can scrape this mousy gerbil nest into a proper bun.

It's not that I care what those who read the Hollywood gossip blogs or the entertainment rags *actually* think; I'd simply rather forgo the maelstrom of negativity. A good presentation before disappearing once again prior to the interview will be a lot smoother. The public will write me off as "living a quiet life and doing well," thereby allowing me to circumvent a feeding frenzy.

Because despite what people might think of such scrutiny, assigning it as merely something that "comes with the territory" of wealth and fame, it's painful nonetheless, and it's an exquisite pain because no matter how much you tell yourself not to take it personally, and how lame you feel for having done so, you can't help but do so.

Big Mike checks on me every couple of minutes until he breaks for good by the emergency room entrance. I pay him with the last twenty in my wallet, and when he gives me the change he says, "You keep me posted if you have the time, all right? And you'll be fine. I've taken a lot worse here. I could tell you some stories!"

"I'll bet." I can't help but laugh.

"You'll be all right!" he calls as I hobble inside to a full waiting room, one seat left.

That qualifies as a miracle if you ask me, not because it actually *is* a miracle, but because I want it to be.

※

After registering at the desk and inwardly thanking the Screen Actors Guild for my health coverage, I sit down, nursing my thigh, encircling it with my hands.

I look right at home with so many of the other inhabitants of the room. In fact, it looks pretty much like every emergency room scene you've ever seen in a movie. The same ragtag patients and their tagalong attendants. The smelly, the scared, the annoying, the quiet, the inappropriately loud, the cell phone talker and the pacer, those who are alone and those who wish they were, all present and accounted for.

When a woman about my age wearing powder-blue sweats and an Ocean City T-shirt snaps my picture with her smart phone, I realize it's all over.

All the plans to beat Jessica to the punch, to plan a "free

and fashionable" comeback, to travel to New York City and stay at the St. Regis, unravel like an unfettered braid. I'm still just Fiona Hume, fallen bad girl and general screwup. That's what they'll say.

And maybe they're right.

Tempting though it is, I don't ask her to refrain from sending it off to that monkey-faced lard-ass Perez Hilton or whatever acid-penning blogger she's dispatching it to right now with a smug, superior grin stretching her closed red lips.

What would be the point?

If not her, someone else. I learned that lesson young.

My father will be snapped at the Baltimore-Washington Airport, various assumptions will be made and repeated as cosmic truth, and I'll retreat once again into the noise and clutter that dangles and flutters in the place of my own making.

✳

Ninety minutes later, still in the waiting room, a text from Jack lights up my screen.

Where are you, Fi?

University.

I'm on my way. Don't leave yet!

I look down at my leg and my grimy pj's.

Don't worry. I'm not going anywhere.

Fourteen

I call Josia's number at the forge and tell him what happened.

"I'll be right there," he says, obviously willing to drop everything.

"No, that's okay. A friend is on his way right now."

My name is finally called and I feel like I've won a contest I was forced to enter.

"I gotta go, Josia. They're finally getting to me."

"Call if you need *anything*, Fia. I'm always around. Keep me posted if you have it in you."

"Thanks, Josia."

As the doctor, a Korean woman in lavender scrubs and pearls, stitches me back together, her slightly nervous chatter informs me she recognizes me but is too professional to mention it.

Thank God.

Which makes me realize with a sense of shame that dressed

normally, I can walk and bike about the city unrecognized. But dress me like a heroin addict who can't get out of her pajamas in the morning or keep from wounding herself by her own abject stupidity, and the resemblance is unmistakable.

I guess you have to come to a place in time where, having kicked everyone to the curb, there's nobody left but yourself to blame if you still haven't moved on.

Let's call that Mount Reality. Because I'm standing on top of it right now.

※

Jack has charmed a nurse's aide into escorting him into the inner sanctum. I can hear his easy voice as they approach the curtain. "I may not technically be family, per se, but I'm all she's got left now." I know he doesn't believe that for a second, and I smile despite the numbing needle going in and out of my thigh.

"Oh, I understand," the aide whispers, tying the laces of conspiracy and pity around her words in hopes of binding herself to Jack in one small way, even for a moment.

He walks into the room dressed in jeans and a baseball shirt, looking beautiful to me.

He sets his cap on the rolling tray table. "I was mid-flight from Lucy's when you called the first time. I came from the airport."

The sight of his face shines the first ray of hope I've had since that woman snapped my picture.

He scoots a chair close to the bed. "Can I see?" he asks the doctor.

"Sure," she says as she continues to stitch.

"Wow, that's bad, Fia."

"And the rake was rusted, so yay," I inform him.

"Don't worry." The doctor looks up. "You'll be getting a tetanus shot."

Yay for that too.

Jack screws up his face. "I hate needles."

"Good thing it's not you on this table," I say. "Thanks for coming right over."

"Of course. When you called . . . well, I'm glad you called."

The doctor cuts the final suture, then begins dressing the wound as we watch, silent. She finishes, stands, and peels off her latex gloves. "I'll have that tetanus shot ordered, and after that you can go. We'll include instructions on changing your bandage, but you'll need to get it looked at again in a few days just to make sure everything's all right."

Beautiful.

She throws the garbage in a pedal-powered trash can, washes up, then leaves the room.

"Wow," Jack says again. "Fia, what happened?"

I run down the agenda of a day that's clearly not living up to what I had in mind. Good thing I made that list.

"And now it's after five, and my father is flying in tonight."

"Oh, geez, Fi. I'm sorry."

"It's okay." The story of the cell phone photographer comes next. "I don't even want to check what's happened since. I mean, look at me."

He takes my hand. "Do you want me to take a peek on Twitter?"

I nod. "I mean, if nothing's there and she just wanted to show her friends or whatever, I could be worrying for nothing."

"True. Okay, hold on a sec." His fingers, long and with neatly trimmed nails, skate across the slick surface of his phone. He types my name across the search strip.

His brows knit together and he sighs. "Well, it's out there already and you haven't even left the hospital."

Amazing, isn't it?

I hate the world sometimes.

"And with my father flying in tonight . . ."

He shakes his head. "What terrible timing."

"To make matters worse, I was going to try to make myself a little more presentable, but here we are at—what time is it, exactly?"

"Five forty-five."

"Five forty-five and he'll be landing in less than two hours."

"Come to my place, Fia. You can stay there while he's in town. He can even stay there too. I'm assuming you want him to think you're doing great."

What he's really saying stings a little, but I can't see any other way around it. There's something comforting about the fact that I haven't fooled him.

"Okay. Let's just swing by my house on the way so I can grab some clothes."

There's simply no other way at this point. No spree with Josia's rent money. Just a trip up to the Hollywood Room and nothing more. I'll manage because I have to.

My tetanus shot administered, instructions and prescriptions handed to me, we exit the hospital and start walking to the small lot where Jack parked the old Porsche he restored himself several years ago. Flashes from three photographers' cameras blind me.

I don't even bother holding up my hand to cover my face. What's the point? It doesn't matter.

You hide; you're found.

You try to shake off those who tail you, you pull off the highway, but if you venture out on the road, even for a second, they'll find you. You just have to use your wits not to let them run you over. This is our world. There is no privacy. And even the illusion of it has wafted away in the breeze of our own morbid curiosity and self-disclosure.

Jack sits me in the passenger seat and hurries to his side of the car. The engine thrums under the turn of his key, and soon we're pulling away. He's practically as smooth as Big Mike.

"Fia, I'm really sorry about all this."

"It's okay. It comes with the territory. I had just forgotten about it. It'll teach me to stay away from rakes, I can tell you that."

"Good policy. It's why I live in a small rowhouse. No leaves. No rakes."

I laugh. It feels good next to him in his car, on terms not exactly of my own making or choosing, granted, but I can choose for it to be okay. And so it's okay. It's more than okay.

A few minutes later he swings onto Mount Vernon Place and I point to my house. "That one there. The haunted one. Just pull up and I'll run in and grab my things."

He says nothing about my big house or its raggedy appearance as he cuts the engine and then circles the vehicle to assist me. "Want me to come in and help you?"

"No!"

"Sorry, sorry."

"That was harsh. I just . . . can't."

"It's okay. Don't rush," he says. "Take your time or you'll open that wound again."

I examine his face, searching for disappointment, horror, disgust, even mild surprise. Nothing's there but good old Jack.

By the time I eke my way inside and grab several changes of clothing from my room and the Hollywood shrine, shove it all into a tote bag, and inch back outside to his car, it's almost seven o'clock.

"Let's get you back," he says after placing my bag in the trunk and resuming his seat behind the wheel. "You can clean up, get ready, and when your dad arrives, we'll make sure he's entertained and happy for his daughter."

"What a scam."

"Hey, you did the same thing for me with Lucy. The least I can do is return the favor."

"Is that what we were doing? Convincing her you're happy?"

He pauses. "Yes. Yes, I guess it was."

Funny how you can misjudge a person's emotional state. "I thought you were happy. You always seem to be."

He slides the car into first gear and pulls away. "Oh, a lot about my life pleases me. I have material comfort, which I never take for granted, a good career, and you know how much I love my house. But it's missing one thing."

And she's sitting next to you in the front seat.

Well, this is new. It has seemed that most of my life I couldn't make anybody happy. And now it appears I am the *one thing* that could make this other person happy.

Either way, it's just too much pressure.

Fifteen

After I wash myself in a sort of standing bath, Jack helps me scrub my hair at the kitchen sink. He takes his time, fingertips going deep into my hair, massaging my scalp.

A little to the right. Left. Up on top. Down the sides. By the nape of my neck. Repeat, repeat, repeat.

"Don't feel you have to go to all that trouble," I say, hoping he won't listen to my advice.

"You need this more than the washing. Man, your muscles are tense."

"Not surprisingly."

His fingertips press circles into the nape of my neck, moving sideways to the depressions behind the lobes of my ears.

"Have you checked Twitter?" I ask.

"Shh. That will keep. Just relax, Fi."

So I do, shifting all my weight onto my right leg, my body leaning into his.

After he's finished, my hair rinsed, conditioned, then rinsed again, he gathers it into a soft, ivory towel and leads me toward the living room.

The sky holds on to the final periwinkle glow of the day outside the sliding glass doors as eight o'clock, and Brandon, approach. Oh, man, I love this town so much. My heart swells at the purple of my city in a dying day. I'm not LA. I'm this right here.

I step forward. "Would you check Twitter?" I ask. "I promise I won't ask again. I just want to know what my father is going to see when he gets off the plane."

He helps lower me down on the sofa, one of those deceptively large affairs that won't let you go from its softness once you descend. A winey red, it's littered with pillows for every purpose. His fingers curl around one of them, a tube of softness for the neck, and set it on the simple white cube of a coffee table in front of us. When he lifts my leg to settle it on top, I want to scream in agony. But there's no way I'm taking those painkillers and risking stepping on that road again. That's way too much pain to experience again. I'd rather go for the quick flare of healing than the slow burn of suffering.

At least I learned that much.

"Do you have any ibuprofen?" I ask.

"Sure thing."

He doesn't ask why because he doesn't have to. He returns with the bottle and a glass of orange juice.

"Thanks."

As I take the pain reliever, he reaches for his phone.

He blows a whistle from his lips. "Wow, Fi, you're obviously not forgotten."

"That bad?" I take the pill.

"Oh, you've still got your defenders out there and they're working overtime."

I rest the glass on my good thigh. "Really?"

"Yes."

"But overall?"

He shuts off the phone's screen. "Do I have to spell it out? I'd rather not."

"Okay. That's probably for the best."

"Trust me on that one. Drink your juice. You don't want to get dehydrated. I assume you lost a lot of blood?"

He's right. I nod and start sipping, but with more intent.

"On the upside," he says with a laugh, "I'm now one of those 'mystery men.'"

"Oh man. I'm so sorry, Jack."

"Don't be. At least my car was clean."

Our laughs join in the presence of his practicality.

"Really, Fia. Don't sweat anything on my account. I can handle it."

"Jack, you don't know what this machine can do."

"Keep sipping, Fi," he says. "Maybe not this particular machine. But I know other machines, and they all basically work the same, gears grinding without a thought as to who gets stuck inside. Machines don't care, and the sooner we all realize that, the better off we are."

"Damn, that's jaded."

"Just realistic."

"You make it sound way easier than it is." I finish the last of the juice, and he takes the glass and sets it on a copy of *Motor Trend* on the coffee table.

"Never easy, but straightforward and predictable."

I shrug. "If you say so. It's never felt that way to me."

My phone rings. "It's my father." I slide the bar across the screen. "Hi, Brandon."

"Fia! Are you all right? Your mother's left five messages on my phone."

I sigh. "I guess you've seen the photo."

"What photo?"

"Twitter?" I ask.

"Fia, I'm too old for all that."

I hate to say it, but good for him.

"I injured myself on a rake in my basement this afternoon. I'll tell you about it when you get here."

"Where's here? I'm about to pick up the rental car."

"I'll text you the address."

"Sounds good. I'll see you when I get there. You sure you're okay?"

I slide my gaze over to Jack. "I'm in good hands. Seriously."

We hang up and I shoot off Jack's address.

"Well, he's on his way," I say.

"Let me help you get ready."

When he helps me to my feet, the stiffening of my muscles pulls a cry from my mouth. He picks me up and carries me up the stairs and into his room. When he sets me on the bed, he says, "Let's get you an outfit from your suitcase."

Twenty minutes later I'm dressed in a full gray skirt, a white cotton blouse freshly ironed by Jack, and because actual outfits weren't on my mind as I stuffed clothing into my suitcase, one of Jack's cardigans, its heathery-brown cashmere hanging almost to my knees.

We roll up the sleeves to just below my elbows.

"Very nice," he says. "Really, Fi. You look pretty."

I eye myself in the mirror on the back of the closet door. Not frumpy. Sort of prep-school girl grown up, and not in a sleazy way either.

"You going to put any makeup on? Not that you need it," he finishes in a rush.

"I don't think so. He knows I spent half the day in the emergency room and half my childhood in a makeup chair."

"Good. Plus, you don't need it anyway."

"You already said that."

"I know."

He gets a comb from the bathroom and hands it to me as I sit down on the edge of the bed. "It's nice that you don't feel you have to completely overhaul yourself for your dad," he remarks.

"My dad doesn't really deserve it."

"Your mom?"

"Well, I'd do it for her just to keep her off my back."

"Ah," he says in his "maybe there's some food for thought there" manner.

When my hair is free of tangles, I ask, "Do you know how to braid?"

He smiles. "Yep. Had a horse when I was little and Lucy had me braid his tail."

"Thanks."

He takes the comb and runs it back from my forehead, its teeth pulling my hair smoothly to where he's gathered a ponytail. "Why do you think your mom called your dad but not you?"

"Because she doesn't really give a damn about me, Jack."

"Or maybe she figured you were a little busy?" He separates the ponytail into three sections.

"Yeah, right."

"Fia, did you ever get along with your mom and dad?"

"Honestly? I feel like I never really knew them."

"That's really sad."

I consider that. It's always pissed me off more than saddened me.

"Maybe I'll put on just a little makeup," I say. "Enough

to hide these dark circles anyway, so I don't look like Captain Quirk. You know, to this day, I don't know how they got Brandon's eyes so hollow looking."

Jack casts me a sad smile. "Fia, what made your dad take on that goofball film role in the first place?"

"I have no idea. Nobody does. He really doesn't like to talk about it. I've always assumed the money was right."

"Hmm."

The doorbell rings.

"I'll go get it," he says, "then come back up and get you."

So I wait on the bed, forgoing the makeup, listening to the warm timbre of male voices greeting each other—Jack's quick explanation that I'll be right down, Brandon's concern, the offer of a drink, the accepting of that drink, and the subsequent clinking of ice cubes from the kitchen.

I pick up my phone and jab the little blue birdie right in the belly.

Why I decided to look at Twitter, I don't know. You would think I would remember exactly what it feels like to be pummeled by the nastiness of others' mindless and ill-informed opinions, but time had somehow blurred the edges of the feeling.

Well, nothing's blurred now.

"Still a loser."

"Oh my god, so fugs!"

"Somebody *try* to make this girl go to rehab. Please!"

And . . .

"For all you haters out there, Fia Hume is still the best actress of all time."

Well, that was nice.

"Shut up everybody. I don't think it's even @FiaHume. She never looked that bad. Stop hating."

Talk about a backhanded compliment.

But right now I'll take it.

I press the button at the bottom of my phone and realize I left Josia in the dark. He probably doesn't even know what Twitter is.

I call the forge and an employee picks up. "He told me you'd be calling, Fiona. Here's his new cell phone number. I never thought I'd see the day he'd get one, but he picked up a throwaway for the next few days. He was that concerned." His voice is soft and kind. I picture a bearded hippie guy who makes his own shoes and eats health food, but would never turn down a milkshake if you were whizzing some up in your blender.

After he gives me the number, I call.

Josia picks up right away. "Fiona! How are you?"

"Okay. All stitched up. I'll be staying with a friend for the next few days."

"Good. You'll need some looking after. Call me anytime if you need anything. I'll have the phone with me at all times."

It's hard to believe someone so new in my life can care this much. And what's even harder to believe is that I not only don't mind this but am glad. It's like I've known him for years. I mean, we say that all the time about people, but every time I've ever said it, and meant it, feels watered down compared to this cup of strong knowing and smooth affection.

"Thanks, Josia. It's good to know somebody is at the house."

"Glad to hold down the fort. Now get some rest." He laughs. "But only if you want to."

"Will do."

Time to face Brandon. I haven't laid eyes on my father for five years.

I decide to make my way down without help.

Jack can't carry me around forever, so the sooner that precedent isn't set, the better.

✳

Grimacing, I rise to my feet, inch across the room carrying that realization, and hop down the steps on my good leg. The hallway seems to have lengthened by at least thirty feet, every step burning. Finally, gripping the wall the entire way, I stand in the doorway to the living room, pale, I assume, a bead of sweat rolling from my hairline, down my temple, and over the side of my cheek. "Wow," I whisper.

Both men look up and my thoughts race through my brain at lightning speed. Somehow, he's here when I need him. My father. I don't know how. The one who backed off almost completely after the divorce is in this living room with his tousled hair, his crooked smile revealing teeth that aren't rivaled in real life, his light-blue eyes. My father who, in hindsight, maybe didn't so much turn his back but instead was licking his wounds outside a room I nailed shut and didn't allow him to enter.

Was that what happened?

Oh please!

Is the trauma causing me to see things in a more benevolent light, and is this light the light of truth? It sure isn't wishful thinking. I can tell you that.

"Fia!" He hurries toward me. "Let me help you."

My first reaction is to bristle and shake my head and hold my hand up in refusal. Then my body sags. The fact is, I need help and, okay, right now would be good. He's only helping me across the room, not setting a precedent forever and ever. "Thanks. I could use it."

My father is tall, but he reduces his height at the knees, sidling in beside me while sliding his arm across my back, his hand curling around my rib cage. The other arm crosses in front of his body, his free hand cupping my elbow.

I press down a sob.

Slowly we traverse the path between pain and a comfort of sorts where Jack is already arranging couch cushions and throw pillows in what appears to be a highly engineered manner. Brandon and I lower my body, and he helps lift my leg onto a pillow that is perfectly positioned to receive my ankle. "Thanks, Jack."

My father sits to my left. "Nice gentleman you have here, Fia. That's good to see."

"Glad she'll put up with me," Jack says. "Have you had dinner yet?" Next subject!

Brandon says, "No. How about I wander next door and see if that restaurant will box us up something?"

"I'll take care of it," Jack says, and all I can think is, *Not yet. Don't leave me here alone with him yet.* He must have seen the panic in my eyes because he says, "It'll only take a few minutes."

"Perfect," Brandon says, sitting next to me. "I didn't want to go out. It has its serious drawbacks."

I can't help but laugh at his dry tone. "Boy, does it. How do you stand it after all these years?"

"Desperation!" he says right away. "I'm an actor, and that's all I'll ever be because I don't have the skills to do anything else."

I know how that feels. I'm living proof of what happens when you stop doing the only thing you're any good at.

"I'll be right back," Jack says, heading toward the coat closet. "Brandon," he calls over his shoulder, "you still a vegan?"

"Never was," Brandon replies. "That was in that film about the man who went to India to learn yoga. I can't remember the title right now."

Jack turns. "I'm sorry, Brandon. I think I missed that one."

"*Bill*," I say. "It was just called *Bill*."

I can sense it doesn't even occur to him that the inability to remember such a simple title might raise a question or two.

Guess he has higher mountains to traverse in the self-examination process. Apparently yoga and veganism aren't among them.

"Did you call Mother?" I ask, thinking another glass of OJ right now would be amazing.

"Yes. She's glad your accident wasn't serious and says she's already called her publicist and they're working overtime to keep any damage from occurring. Her next film releases in a month. Not to mention that book."

"I'm sure you're not going to look good after that thing comes out," I say.

He grins. "Fia, I've never been seen out there as a good person. I'm a good actor who appears to be having fun with his life and trying not to really hurt anybody. But I'm not admired for my character and my courage."

"You're no Angelina Jolie?"

He laughs. "Nope. I try to keep whatever I do for the good a little more secret."

"But why?"

"I don't think the people I help need to be seen as the people I helped. They're proud. And they should be."

"Who are you talking about?"

"Guess that's for me to know and you to find out."

"Assuming you'll stick around that long," I say. And where is that OJ?

"That's not for me to say," he reminds me.

"So Mom is doing damage control. What about you?"

He sips his tonic water (Brandon's big into the AA thing) and then sets it on the same magazine I used earlier. Things like Jack's lack of coasters go far in assuring me he's not gay, and although he tries hard, he's not fully equipped, like most men on the planet, to create a fully equipped home. Why this is, I can't say. Nevertheless, you can't say I'm wrong, can you?

"What do you mean, what about me?" he asks.

"Have you called your publicity person?"

He barks out a laugh. "I don't even remember her name."

"Really?"

"Fia, that's for my manager to handle. I just want to be told where and when to show up and make the decision whether I want to do the movie in the first place. That's it."

"But you used to—"

"That was a long time ago."

"Can you pour me a glass of OJ?" I ask.

I've never seen Brandon's eyes look more pleased than they do right now as he nods, says, "Absolutely, of course," and heads toward the kitchen.

※

To understand the Atlantic Ocean that separates my feelings for Brandon and how he is acting, sitting here in Jack's row-house being all sweet and concerned, one would have to go back to my older childhood.

Later, I tell Jack this up in the bedroom after a dinner of fried clams, onion rings, coleslaw, and carrot cake. He pats the bed. "Get off that leg," he decrees, then hands me a glass of water and the next round of ibuprofen.

"I figured there has to be an explanation," he says. "Your dad seems pretty laid-back. I like him."

"He's an actor," I say. I swallow the pills.

"True enough. But I'd like to think I'm shrewd enough to tell the difference."

"You do deal with a lot of people." I nod.

"Too many."

"Did I seem really bitter?" I ask.

"You're an actor, Fi."

Well, that smarts a little.

"So tell me." He sits on his side of the bed. "What was he like?"

I eye the open door. He hops up and shuts it. "Okay, go ahead."

"First of all, you had a good relationship with your parents, right?"

He nods. "Yes." Jack's dad died ten years ago, when he was twenty-five.

"So I'm not sure how much of this you can even understand, but okay, imagine the most bad-boy actor you can think of—drunken binges, womanizing, spending money like it would just wash up on the beach and lay itself at your feet. Then picture someone like Richard Burton."

"Fi, it seems to me you just described Richard Burton."

"Alec Guinness, then."

"Much better."

"Then combine the two."

He grins. "Why don't I just picture Richard Burton?"

He does fill all the necessary requirements on his own. "Good point. Okay, so just picture Richard Burton, but prep school, beer pong–style American. Kinda like an old frat boy who's really good at acting."

"Ah, got it."

"Now imagine that man marries a narcissist, one of the most beautiful women in the world." I lean forward. "Let that fact sink in a second. In fact, if you let it sink in while getting me a glass of orange juice, so much the better."

He laughs. "You got it."

Believe it or not, this is the first adult conversation I've had about my parents, ever. Other than with therapists, but that's just not the same. Lila and I talked a lot about our lives, but she was as messed up as I. She wasn't a grown-up like Jack.

He returns with the juice.

"Thanks." I take the glass and sip. "Have you ever dealt with a narcissist?" I ask him.

"Sure. They're everywhere."

"Well then, they could take lessons from my mother."

He takes a sip of my juice. And not a huge one either. I like that about Jack. He never presumes. "So she played the martyr and talked about it all the time, thereby poisoning you against your father and making him the reason for her unhappiness?"

Dang, he's perceptive.

"Uh . . . yeah? Wow."

"And then made *you* responsible for her happiness," he finishes.

"That's right."

"I was a psychology major too, Fia." He pulls down the comforter and fluffs the pillows. "Was it true, that they mishandled your earnings?"

"Yes." I appreciate what he's doing, but the thought of even swiveling over to get into bed seems very Everesty. "I said it was their financial manager, but Brandon couldn't keep his hands off of it, and Jessica was content to let him because it allowed her to keep playing the victim. She tends to like to keep things as they are."

"Ah. Which is why she continues to stay with him."

"And why I had to get them out of my life as much as possible."

"When did your dad stop drinking?" he asks.

"After our divorce was final."

"A little too late, huh?"

"Yeah. Exactly."

I yawn, the accumulation of the day's events fully collected into a need for sleep.

He pats my good leg. "I'll let you go to bed. Thanks for telling me this, though. I know it's hard."

"You've proven your trustworthiness, Jack."

He just stares at me, then gets up and walks into the dressing room. I hear a drawer open, close a few seconds later, then another one. He emerges with a small stack of clothing, what appears to be a clean T-shirt and boxers. Heavy socks too.

"All right," he says, "I'll see you in the morning," and heads toward the bedroom door.

"You're not going to sleep in here?"

"Fi, I have to live on my terms now, not yours. I've given what I could under the circumstances and played along with your game at the risk of my own dignity. But now that the truth is out, the old rules are over. I'm going to treat you like the lady I've always thought you are. The fact is, I don't have to pay for friendship and a little making out. I never have. I just did what I needed to do to take care of you. Now you can either accept that or not. But I'm not paying for you anymore. The business arrangement is over. I'll help you and support you as your friend, and if anything else develops, I'll be happy. But if it doesn't, then it doesn't, and at least I know I respected you the best way I knew how. And what is more, I respected myself."

Jack can handle this no other way. If he could, I'd have lost all respect for him.

"Good night," he says, leaving the bedroom and closing the door behind him.

Sixteen

It's only six thirty. The sun has not yet gained the horizon, but the sky begins to hold on to its light, pulling itself up from indigo to the hushed pearl gray of early morning.

Baltimore is beginning to stir, the black streets increasing their usefulness, clocking in for the commuter traffic. Some of the nearby residents walk their dogs by the water. Others jog or clip along at a stiff walk, oblivious, or so it seems, to the calm water of the harbor.

I'm sitting on Jack's rooftop deck, snuggled in an ivory robe, my leg throbbing in time to every car that rolls by below with the volume pumped up on its stereo. But even with this, I realize for the first time in years I'm exactly where I want to be. Not even where I'm supposed to be, but where I'd choose to be if given a choice in the matter.

The men are asleep, and my conversation with Jack keeps

rolling around in my thoughts and, I suspect, deeper down. As I gained and lost consciousness throughout the night, I could only think about Brandon, and what it must have been like to be married to Jessica all those years.

I hear the doors open behind me and cross my fingers, still gazing outward.

Jack sits down next to me. Good.

I look at him and smile as he hands me a cup of coffee. He returns the grin, but we say nothing, sitting together in our matching bathrobes. We watch as the sky continues to lighten, each new shade snipping at the time left until Brandon will stir. Despite his lifestyle back in the old days, he never slept in past eight. And even so, he was all bathrobes, smoothies, brisk swims, and catching up on the news at that time of day.

"What are you thinking about?" he asks.

"My father."

"Makes sense."

"It's like this, Jack. I'm not going to rewrite history and pretend he was the world's greatest dad. He sucked. He was never home. But who would want to hang around a woman like Jessica? A woman who thought, because of her beauty and prestige, she was laying a privilege on you if she deigned to breathe the same air as you?"

"A father whose daughter needs him there?"

"I see your point. But I know *I* don't want to be around that. To this day."

We sip our coffees halfway down as the streets below continue to heat up.

"Is there a place deep down that can learn to love my dad a little bit?" I continue. "He's adventurous and generous these days, respected and adored, despite what he says. And there's a reason for that."

"Can you trust him?" Jack asks.

"I just don't know."

"Maybe that's what all of this is for, Fi. You know?"

I laugh. "You sound like Randi at the coffee shop!"

"Just thinking out loud."

"Jack?"

"Yes?"

"You know those movies about noble people, or rich people, or even movie stars, where the mother and father pawn their kids off on a nanny and a kind domestic staff?"

"Like *The Great Gatsby*?"

"Yes, exactly. And they have certain times of the day where their gorgeous parents visit them and fawn over them for a little bit. They sing a little song or play patty-cake, and then they leave the nursery to enjoy a fabulous dinner in their glittering dining room, or go out to whatever beautiful, glittering activity they have planned?"

"Yes," he says. "And the children always seem so well adjusted and happy."

"Amazingly so." I sink my hands in the pockets of my robe.

"Well, it isn't like that. Because the times in between seem so long, and they don't show how the kids look upon their parents as foreign objects to their *real* world. They don't show that after a while, the children grow further and further away, forgetting the umbilical cord completely. They resent that they are at their parents' convenience, their schedules revolving around that brief time of interaction that becomes more and more meaningless, more pointless, as the years roll on."

"I can see that. It sounds horrible."

"Soon enough, the child, most likely around puberty, begins to suspect something is not only highly amiss, but deeply wrong with the arrangement because they watch enough television to realize most parents don't interact with their children that way."

"I can see that too." He swings his legs to the side of his chaise and takes my hand.

I want to pull away, but his hand feels so warm and comforting. The feel of his fingers entwining with my own sets off a great honking alarm at the base camp of my skull, but still I cannot pull away. He only wants me, Fia. All of me, yes, but nothing more than that, and nothing less.

"Go on, Fi," he says.

"Well, the parents figure it's finally time to step in and assert authority they didn't care to develop along the way. They demand respect and obedience, thinking it's a right they automatically have, not a privilege they've earned because they were there for that child all along."

I pause, remembering the screaming fights with Jessica from thirteen until the final decree of divorce three years later. She'd always cry, "How can you *do* this to me, Fiona?"

"Brandon, to his credit, stayed away." I finish the thought out loud. "That was the decree of the courts."

"An apology might have been nice," he says, squeezing my hand. And wow, yes, the man is on my side. Not because I'm right or have a just cause, but because he decided to be there.

I'm not used to this kind of person. Clearly.

I shrug. "It's hard to know if that would have made any difference by that point."

"I think it might have," he says.

"You're probably right. After the divorce, Brandon settled down a little bit, but he threw himself even more into his work and tried to hide the fact that he was so wounded by the entire situation."

"I remember. Your mom was a piece of work for a while there too."

"'The lady doth protest too much.'"

"It didn't matter, though, Fia. There isn't a person alive who sees a divorce situation like that and fails to blame the parents. They were the *parents*, for God's sake."

"It's true. But you know what, Jack? Even when all is said and done, you still don't have a mom and dad."

"Fia, I'm sorry. Can I sit next to you on your chair?"

The simple question brings tears to my eyes, and I slide

over with a wince. He sits on the side of my lounger, reaches forward, and tucks my hair behind my ear. "But you're here now," he says. "And your father's in there, and you've kinda been thrown together for the next few days."

"Believe me. I know."

"What's your gut telling you to do with this?"

"Nothing. It's telling me to just roll with whatever comes along."

"Is that even possible?" he asks. "With that leg and all?" His eyes twinkle.

"I don't know. But I'm willing to see."

He leans forward and kisses me on the cheek. "I'll get you some juice."

After I give myself a sponge bath, Jack checks on my leg and changes the dressing. I feel like I've been on a shoot for twelve hours, every scene consisting of nothing but running down a long corridor or across an airplane hangar. Still no word from Jessica, although Jack told me he heard Brandon talking to her last night after I went to bed, doing nothing but placating her. He probably knows all the right things to say at this point without using up any emotion whatsoever. I'm sure she's all over Twitter asking for prayers and "good thoughts" for me and the family. And as bad as this leg feels, I'm reasonably sure she's making it seem far worse. I'm probably in danger of losing it, according to social media. And I ran into that rake because I was either falling down drunk or tripping my ass off, for sure. Not that she'll tweet that. But she won't say anything to the contrary. Substance abuse makes for a much more exciting story, and exciting stories, even though they're unacknowledged by the supposed players, sell movie tickets.

And copies of books.

She's got to be giving herself multiple high fives at the timing of all this.

Jack walks into the bedroom to check on me. "You doing okay? You look nice."

"Thanks." I grip my gray wool skirt. "You know what? People are always searching for the truth, and I'm wondering if all that even matters anymore."

"Wow. I leave you for fifteen minutes and look what happens." He laughs.

"Seriously, Jack." I pat the spot next to me on the bed and he sits down.

"So what brought this on?" he asks.

"Social media."

"You didn't go checking, did you?"

"I don't have to."

"*That's* the truth." He *hmm*s. "So that's what brought about these thoughts?"

"Yes! Nowadays people formulate truth; they don't find it.

I'm sure people have opinions about what happened to me even though none of them have heard about it from me. And you know what's even sicker?"

"They're so sure about it?"

"Right! So I ask you. If this is what happens with the situation of someone who is, truly, as insignificant as I am, how can we possibly know, really and truly know, what is going on with what *really* matters?"

"We can't. Not about all the big stuff. Halls of Congress, international affairs. Is that what you mean?"

"Exactly. The everyday Joes, like you and me, a lot of them know nothing firsthand and think they know everything. And they talk-talk-talk-talk and post their opinions all over the Internet and it's loud and ridiculous. It's like we're all in this ship of fools and nobody knows if the boat is even real."

Jack looks at me. Really looks at me.

"What we have, Fia, is right now. And the job we have before us, and the people in front of us. That's all we can hope is real. And even then . . ."

"You don't even know what those people are really thinking."

He nods. "And sometimes for the best of reasons."

"And then there's my mom."

"Yep."

I start to stand and he helps me to my feet. "So, bearing what you said in mind, I guess the overall answer is to find what you love to do and do it, and hold close and be good to the people you love?"

He tucks my arm in his. "And let them love you in return."

"Why does that sound so hard?"

Placing his hand over mine, he says, "Because you have to be honest with yourself to do it."

Seventeen

Brandon, chipper and concerned, seems to have had a good night's sleep, if looking like a leading man in a pair of old boxers and a ratty JHU T-shirt is any indication.

He sits at the dinette and pours himself a glass of juice. "Well, I've officially turned off my phone. I told my agent and manager that we're all doing fine, nobody's dying, and they'd better damn well handle it because I'm not only paying them for the good times."

"Well done," says Jack. He offers to make us breakfast but both Brandon and I refuse. I get my weak morning stomach from him.

"So what's on the agenda for today?" Jack asks Brandon, refreshing my coffee, no space-age crystals included.

"I have the benefit luncheon at noon, a cocktail photo op

session at four, a little schmoozing afterward with the really big donors, and then I'll be back."

"And I'm useless now," I say, pointing to my leg, not stating the obvious fact that I'm thrilled I don't have to appear in public. Terrible way to get there, but since I'm here, might as well appreciate at least one of the outcomes.

Brandon winces. "Never useless, Fia. Think of how much better it will all be knowing I can come back and hang with you."

I smile. I can't help it. So does Jack.

"We'll plan a nice time. Right here," he says. "Because I have a feeling you won't be going anywhere today, Fia."

"I have a feeling you're right about that." What in the world am I going to do with myself all day?

An hour later Brandon is off in a rented Saab and Jack has left to run out to the country for some meeting with clients trying to make their next factory as close to zero emissions as possible. Not only do I not have the Schwinn, but even if I did, I only have one usable leg to power it with.

Oh, boo-hoo, Fiona.

I decide the upper deck is still the best option, and so I grab a book—speaking of *The Great Gatsby*—and a bottle of water and plant my bottom on what now feels like my own lounge chair.

At eleven my phone rings.

Oh joy! Jessica.

I knew it had to happen; I could feel it coming like rain in the tropics, but some spark of hope that it wouldn't neverthe-less had remained ignited. Until this drowning moment.

There's no help for it. She'll keep calling over and over until I answer her. That's her way.

So much for divorce. While Brandon crept away, Jessica still did her best to pounce.

"Hi, Mother."

"Well, you picked a fine time to have an accident, Fiona. I've been doing damage control ever since, but I think you'll end up looking all right."

I'm actually stunned. I mean, Jessica, being an utter narcis-sist, is the queen of the turnaround, and I only know all this due to hours and hours of therapy and reading. But this has got to be her greatest one yet.

"Are you there?" she says. "Did you not hear what I said?"

I bolster myself with one of those cleansing breaths you see on yoga shows. "I think so. But let me repeat it back to you just so I'm sure I've got it. I accidently ripped my thigh open on a rusty rake, called a cab and made it to the emergency room, got my picture snapped by a bystander who then sent it to a blogger who got it out on the Internet, and assumptions were made. And since you have a movie set to release, not to mention your little tell-all, you used it to the fullest to get your name out there and garner all kinds of sympathy without calling me once personally to see how I was doing, and I'm supposed to be fall-ing down at your feet in *gratitude*? Is that right?"

She doesn't miss a beat. "I figured you'd have this kind of reaction. You have no idea what I go through because of you. For sixteen years I've had to bear the stigma of you divorcing us. I will always be seen as an inept mother because of you. The fact that I care at all, much less call you, is amazing forgiveness on my part, and you just refuse to see it."

I lost all hope of Jessica ever changing years ago. "Well, I'm sorry for the inconvenience I've caused you. But I'm in a lot of pain right now."

"Surely they gave you pain meds, Fiona."

"Mom, I'm not going to take them. I can't afford to risk it."

"Well, at least Brandon is there. Although the timing was nothing more than sheer luck on his part."

She's a one-woman show in the theater of the absurd, isn't she?

As for my dad's timing, maybe it was, maybe it wasn't. I'm starting to wonder if there isn't a bigger picture of things at play all around us that I've never really been aware of before now.

"Whatever the reason, he's here and it's going pretty well, so I'm glad." That should have hit the mark, whatever the mark even is with her. I've stopped trying to make so much as a guess at that one. "Anyway, I'd better go. I'm really tired."

"Well, I'm thinking about coming soon. To help you with your recovery."

And without waiting for my good-bye, she immediately ends the call.

Oh no! Oh, hell no, she is *not* coming to Baltimore. She is not coming to my town.

I immediately dial Josia.

"I thought you might want an update," I say after his greeting washes over me like a fountain of peace. How does he do that?

"You thought right," he says, his voice coming through more clearly than usual.

"Everything okay at the house?"

"It's good. Good. Now, are you sure you're fine about the kitchen?"

"Absolutely. Do whatever you want."

"Carte blanche? You're certain?"

"I am. I've been doing a lot of thinking these past twenty-four hours. What you did with your space is more than beautiful, and you work with what you've got on hand."

"I've always found that for the most part, what's on hand is usually enough. Sometimes more than enough. You provided it, Fia. The crib ends, the books, the toys. Don't you see?"

"See? That's what I'm talking about, Josia. And I'm sure there's definitely more than enough at our house."

"How are you holding up?"

"I'm in a lot of pain, but I'm just sitting around for the most part so it's okay."

"No, Fia. I was talking about the publicity."

"You know?"

"Of course."

"But I thought you had no idea."

"Who you are?" He chuckles. "No. I recognized you right away. You were a fine actress, probably still are if you want to know and accept the truth of the matter. I'm sure it's like any other innate talent."

Thankfully there are no paparazzi on this deck to snap a picture of my open mouth. "Why didn't you say anything?"

"Your past makes no difference to me."

The matter-of-factness of his tone implies nothing but sincerity.

"And why should it?" I respond. "I mean, you're right. It really doesn't make a difference. You live your life, go about your day, run your forge, fix up the house, and I used to be a pill-head nympho, and never the twain shall meet."

"Pretty good deduction there. Good."

"I mean, why should I think I'm that important to the whole damn world?" I gaze out over the harbor, happy that my self-description didn't shock him one bit. No shock. Not even pity. Just acceptance. This is new.

The late-May temperatures are solidly in the midseventies now, and the lunch crowd is just beginning to tunnel out of the nearby businesses in search of a meal. And boy, do they have choices around here.

My past makes no difference to them either. While there might have been some watercooler chitchat among those who care about the lives of famous entertainers and sports stars, none of them are going to live their lives any differently because I quit my job, went to rehab, and then quit my job for good. The latest round of news regarding Fiona Hume isn't even going to affect what they put on their forks at dinnertime tonight. I have nothing to do with what shoes they're choosing to put on their feet or how much they're willing to pay for a good cup of coffee.

Maybe one day, long ago, I helped people my age foster really bad choices. I can see what a terrible role model I was. But those days are gone, right?

None of it is true anymore. Ten years is a long time. Ten years of obscurity throws the ball firmly in the other person's court. It's on their own heads now.

"Why did I think I was that important to people?"

"Oh, you were in the sense that you kept people from thinking about their own lives."

"Beautiful. So I provided a distraction. What about the role-model thing?" Might as well get his take on it while we're on a roll.

He laughs. "Fia, it's okay. Just remember that if it hadn't been you, it would have been someone else. It speaks every bit as much about the people themselves, the people who are just looking for an excuse to do what they wanted to do anyway. It's not your job to judge them for doing that."

"I guess you're right."

"Good. It all comes down to what we choose to do. Now, there are some whose choices are forcefully removed from them, and that breaks our hearts. But you didn't do that to anybody."

He's right about that. "If you say so."

"Well, I'd better let you go. Don't want to tire you out. When's your follow-up appointment?" he asks.

"Day after tomorrow."

"You need a lift?"

Not knowing either Jack's or Brandon's schedule, I say, "I'm not sure."

"Let me know if you do."

Ten minutes later I look over the edge of the deck, and somehow, only God could know how, they've found me. A group of photographers and reporters stand waiting around their cars, chatting it up, hoping I'll have to come outside.

Beautiful. Just beautiful.

❀

Jack left me the number for the restaurant next door with instructions to order anything I want for lunch. I inch my way into the kitchen to retrieve the slip of paper from the counter as well as the menu sitting next to it. There in big red letters at the bottom sits my full-fledged relief in the words FREE DELIVERY.

Take that, paparazzi-type people.

Not wanting to take advantage of Jack's kindness or to give myself a reason to owe him even more than I already do, I go simple. The blood I lost left behind a craving for red meat, so a hamburger will do nicely. And with a side of "secretly seasoned shoestring fries," how can I go wrong? And how does one "secretly season" something? Is the seasoning a secret or does one of the kitchen staff, and nobody knows who, sneak in during the night and season the fries with no one the wiser? I can't help it. I laugh out loud at the thought, and man, does that feel good. When I call, I make sure to order the fries just the way they are described. "I'll take a hamburger, medium-rare, and a large order of secretly seasoned shoestring fries."

"Fifteen minutes," the order taker says without hesitation, a very busy kitchen speaking into the phone with him.

"I'll be waiting." Especially for those secretly seasoned fries of yours.

"Sorry, but our delivery guy was a no-show today. You'll have to come pick it up yourself."

Seriously?

"Do you all have a back entrance?" I ask. I should just cancel the order, but those secretly seasoned fries have quickly become an obsession.

"Yeah, why?"

"Those reporters and all out there? I've got a phobia of strangers and—"

"Oh, yeah, yeah, yeah. Sure. Come on in through the alley. I'll just say you're a friend of mine."

I love this town of nice people and mysterious fried food.

In the span of a second, I weigh the option of pain and hot

food vs. a bowl of cold cereal and a lounge chair. And believe it or not, I feel the weight of all my past decisions come raining down to settle in a set of golden scales that fills my mind-screen like a PowerPoint presentation, and not a very good one at that.

One side is filled with all my poor choices, the other is dangling there with just a few ingots, and only one of those is proactive and not simply reactive in a good way. That decision, LET JOSIA REDO YOUR DWELLING, glows in my picture in shiny gold letters.

So I can continue to let life and people come to me, eat whatever crap happens to be at hand, in both the literal and the figurative, or I can risk a lot of pain for the nutrition I need.

"Tell you what," I say into the phone. "Scratch that order. I think I'll just walk down and eat in the dining room." Secret fries don't have to be consumed secretly, do they?

"Okay. Sorry about that." For some reason his voice makes me think of a lot of people on a sofa, all smoking cigarettes.

"No worries. Thanks for your time."

So, okay. Now that the euphoria of decision making has passed, I need to implement the necessary steps between myself and those fries.

I stand over my suitcase and bemoan my quick-draw packing the day before. Then again, Jack's closet could be a treasure trove. But even slipping in the back of the restaurant doesn't mean a photographer won't go in for lunch all on his own, so the pains are necessary. For truthfully, I just want all this to go away. Maybe I can somehow set the record straight and get some protein all in one go. That would be a nice change of pace from being a hermit.

Oh, who am I kidding? They'll all find something to make fun of me for. But does that matter? Granted, it shouldn't, but does it?

In the grand scheme of the universe, not one bit.

I can almost hear the word *good* coming out of Josia's mouth and straight to my ear.

The alleyway is the ticket. I don't need to play this game.

Then again, that attitude is what got me in trouble in the first place.

I stand inside Jack's closet and am freshly impressed by his shirt collection. I grab one of his tank-top undershirts and a freshly starched spread-collar shirt of cotton so soft I'll probably just go ahead and sleep in it and wear it again tomorrow. With my gray skirt and black flats, it should look at least slightly planned. And having entered the inevitable menswear phase when I was twenty, that should not come as a big surprise.

By one o'clock, I slowly climb down the steps to the first floor, my bad leg stiffer than a Buckingham Palace guard. I stand in the hallway, the back door of Jack's house and the front door both visible with a swivel of my head. Something ignites inside of me. I do believe I've finally had enough.

Enough of Mother, my father, and myself.

Just like that.

Is that how this really works?

Don't question it, Fia! Just go with the flow of it. Like you said you would!

So I head straight out the front door and am at once amazed by the bombardment of people yelling my name and snapping pictures. I only expected a few would find this worth their while. My error is both delightful and horrifying at the same time. At least twelve people assemble.

I remember my signature gesture of a peace sign and immediately discard it on the junk heap of tired-out images. Instead, and don't ask me where this is coming from, I hold my hand up like the Queen of England and smile, thankful I remembered to throw in my makeup bag when I packed.

And in that smile, and the gracious replies to questions being lobbed my way, I tell my mother regarding her meddling about in the world of my publicity, "Thanks but no thanks. Ever again."

"Is it true you injured yourself due to inebriation?"

I suddenly recall my role as a teenager ridiculed and bullied and how the character overcame it by throwing herself into her ballet. Yeah, I know. A ballet movie. But she was, and still continues to be, an inspiration to anyone who watches the film. I let her embody me for just a split second to remember what it feels like to be empowered enough to be yourself.

"Not true at all."

"Why were you in the emergency room?"

I can actually tell where this voice is coming from. Tony. The politest one of the bunch, he followed me around for three years.

"Tony!" I shield my eyes against the sun of a zero-humidity afternoon. "How are you?"

Everyone chuckles.

"Long time, no see!" someone shouts.

"Hi, Fiona," Tony says. "Good to see you again."

He always did have a nice smile. And he still wears his signature black Jack Purcells, jeans, and a fitted black T-shirt.

"Likewise. Did you fly all the way from LA?"

He grins. "Took the red-eye just for you."

I laugh and run my fingers along my temple. "You've got some gray in there now. Looks good."

He laughs. "Thanks."

"Then let me answer your question."

Two more photographers run up to stand in front of me. My skin prickles underneath my clothing as my face heats up and my leg begins to throb. Mostly men, dressed comfortably but nice, raise their cameras to their faces. Two women, one a redhead with a propensity for denim, the other with a classic bun and black clothing, do the same.

"I'll pose for pictures in a sec," I say. "But I really want you to listen to what I have to say."

The cameras lower as my gravity is raised.

"Do you mind if I sit down? This leg smarts."

I head over toward a bench by the restaurant's front door. Tony runs up and offers his arm. "Let me," he says.

"Thanks." I curl my fingers around his forearm and pull in close, using his side for support.

"It's good to see you, Fiona," he whispers.

"After all these years," I whisper back. "You were always nice, Tony."

"I always tried to balance the scales for you."

It's true. Nobody took better pictures of me than Tony.

"Why?"

"It's my way."

"Well, it's a nice way."

We reach the bench. I let go, turn around, and lower myself to the seat. "I hurt my leg, you see," I say. "Go ahead and take some pictures and then I'll talk."

For the next thirty seconds, I smile for the crew, lifting my skirt a tad to show the bottom edge of my bandage.

"All right. I was in my basement looking for a shovel. I'm relandscaping my back garden."

"By yourself?" the classy woman asks.

"Mostly. A friend is helping me out there." Pandora's Box sits in front of them, and they smell the fragrance of a new story coming from within. Whether it's a stench or not is up to me.

"The man upstairs?" Tony asks.

"Now there's a hottie," says a photographer.

I laugh. "No. Not him. A very true friend. Anybody have one of them?"

They laugh.

"Anyway, I lost my balance stepping over something. Yes, my basement is very basementy, and a rusted rake tine split open my thigh."

"So you weren't drunk?" asks a younger man dressed in khakis and hiking boots.

"You're new in following me, aren't you?" I ask.

The veterans laugh.

"Alcohol wasn't my problem. And I haven't touched anything stronger than ibuprofen in ten years."

"Even for that?" the other woman asks, pointing to my thigh.

"No. I'm not taking any chances. I'm living a very boring life these days, and I find it's the life for me."

Really? Is this true? Two months ago I was as miserable as I was ten years ago. But the answer fits.

"Care to tell us more about your present life, Ms. Hume?" Tony asks.

"Not today. I'm in pain and I'm hungry. I've got an exclusive interview scheduled in July, so stay tuned. So if you'll excuse me, I'm heading into that restaurant right there to eat some secretly seasoned fries." I struggle to a standing position, trying not to laugh.

"A few more pics?" someone, I can't quite tell who, asks.

"Sure."

And I let them take as many as they want. Finally, "Now go make some money off of this."

We laugh together as the disassembly commences.

That wasn't so bad, even though I forgot lipstick.

Tony helps me inside. The first members of the lunch crowd take note.

"It's good to see you doing well," he says while I wait at the podium for the host to seat me.

"Despite the leg."

"Yes, there's that. Do you ever plan on going back into acting?"

"Oh, definitely not!"

"You were good." He adjusts the shoulder strap of his camera bag. "That's a real shame."

"Is it, though? There are a lot of good actors out there."

The hostess appears. I put out my hand. "Thanks, Tony."

"For what?" He shakes my hand.

"You've always treated me decently."

"Shouldn't everybody?"

"Ha!"

He grins, exposing teeth that would have benefited from orthodontia, but not much. "Yeah, I know."

The hostess steps up to the podium. Her mouth drops open. "Two for lunch?" she stammers.

I look at Tony. "Why not? You hungry?"

He hesitates and I know why. He'll lose this scoop.

"It's okay," I say. "I totally get it."

"You know what? No. No, I don't care. Let's have lunch."

I turn to the hostess. "Two for lunch, then."

She slides two menus off of the stack. "Follow me, please."

Tony offers me his arm. I take it, hearing the click of a camera behind us.

"Would you like to sit outside on the patio?" the hostess asks halfway through the restaurant.

Yes, outside sounds just right.

Eighteen

It's nice when tables turn as they have between Tony and me. Out here in the benevolent May afternoon, the only thing that separates us from the harbor is a stainless steel fence, the handrail too low to obscure my view of the water.

So I ask about Tony's life and realize as he answers that he's just as I suspected. Normal. Compassionate.

"I wish sometimes I wasn't so good at what I do," he says after telling me about his wife and his special needs child. "Gloria bears the brunt of all that with my traveling."

"Why not just be a photographer in . . ." I circle my hand.

"Florence, Mississippi."

Not what I expected.

"Okay. In Florence."

"Nothing there would pay the medical expenses like this does."

And he gave up the scoop to accept my invitation. An idea

comes to mind. "When this leg heals, do you want to do an exclusive shoot and interview?"

He raises his eyebrows.

I nod for emphasis. I might be throwing away that great interview in New York, but who cares about those bigwigs? They don't need me one bit. I'm the one who needed them. "You've always been so kind to me, Tony. Even when I was at my worst."

I regret to say I actually pushed him off his feet when I was eighteen.

"If you find yourself ready for that. Then yes. Of course."

I ask him more questions over lunch—a hamburger for me, poached salmon for Tony—and realize afresh how much more there is to people than simple sight allows, and so far, I've not taken the time to realize that with anybody. I've been guilty of the same mind-set as everybody I've complained about so bitterly.

❋

Josia picks up on the second ring. "Fia!"

"Major breakthroughs going on over here." I tell him about my day so far.

"So I take it you don't have a new boyfriend?"

"The photographer?"

"Already on that tweety thing. Been checking for you."

"No. Tony's . . ." I think for a second. "Well, he's a friend. A friend I didn't know I had, but now I do."

"Good!"

"Kinda like you, Josia."

"Oh, we're everywhere." He laughs.

"Otherwise, how does it look out there?"

"Some believe your story. Others don't. But more do believe than don't now since the lunch pictures, so that's at least an improvement. And the pictures look very nice. You're very photogenic."

"Well, that's better than I expected. How's the kitchen coming?"

"It's good."

"Very good?"

"I'll let you be the judge of that."

Of course he'd say that.

❊

Brandon looks five years older than he did when he left this morning.

"That bad?" I ask as he lowers himself into the lounge chair next to me on the upper deck. A couple of birds have alighted onto the railing, their silhouettes dark against the water reflecting the golden sun of early evening. The heaviest commuter traffic is over, but Baltimore is still mostly making its way home for the night. I love this time of day.

"Oh dear." He blows out a whoosh of air. "I'm happy to help, but heaven help me, Fia. I'm so sick of hearing quotes from *Galaxy Goons* I could scream sometimes."

He slips his feet from his loafers, stretches his legs out in front of him, and for a reason I don't know, his sock feet look very dad-like.

He laughs. "Yep. Well, I'm going to take a shower and wash off the tired."

Oh yeah. "I forgot you say that!"

He smiles, and it's tender and paternal. And something, a seed, a spark, I don't know exactly, stirs within me, and I feel like I want to cry.

❋

"The fact of the matter is that I did to Brandon what the world did to me."

I tell Jack this as he sits in the lounge chair Brandon just occupied, the evening breeze now sweeping in across our faces. I feel like I have my own salon these days where beautiful men come to spend time with me.

"Where is he?" Jack asks.

"Taking a shower."

"So what did you mean?"

"Okay, so I never actually listened to *him*. I let everybody else tell me who he was, what he was up to, why he did what he did, and on and on. Chiefly my mother, and who would choose to believe her? Me, that's who, I guess."

"He could have volunteered up more info, Fia. Not have allowed you to be swayed by the *National Enquirer.*"

"I know."

"I guess you'll just have to ask him. But you should. Sometimes being too nice isn't necessarily the best thing. If he needs to answer for some things, let him. He'll be better off for it."

"I hate conflict like that."

"It will be over soon enough. But my advice? Do it. He may actually want to explain himself and, at the very least, apologize. Did the terms of the divorce keep him from legally doing so before?"

"Basically, yes."

"Well, there you go, then. Now's your chance to find out his side of the story. I'm going to shower and change." He stands up. "Hey, you want something to drink when I'm done?"

"Sure. Surprise me, and then tell me how your day went."

"Well, it was fine until I realized I have some competition out there now." He places his hand on the sliding door handle. "Who was that guy?"

"The nicest member of the paparazzi there is. It was time I took him to lunch. Or rather, *you* took him to lunch."

Jack laughs, seeming relieved. "Fia, you're priceless. And I mean that in the best possible way."

❀

I love watching the harbor from my little crow's nest here on the roof, happy hours going on down beneath me. And who can blame all of the people imbibing? Life is hard. We try to pretend it isn't, or it shouldn't be, at the very least, and then feel guilty for not being able to sail on our life like it is a sea of glass. I remember Elena saying, "Instead of feeling bad that we struggle, we should accept the workings of the universe and congratulate ourselves for making it through another day."

She was always so right about these sorts of things.

Jack hands me a tonic and orange juice and lowers himself on his lounger with a, "Whew, that was a day and a half."

"You smell nice."

"Thanks. But I'm beat."

Because Jack doesn't need a person to pry information out of him like I do, he proceeds to ramble on about the difficulties of his current project. "Every so often I have a client who just doesn't understand what I'm saying no matter how I try to break it down."

"So that's your specialty?" I ask.

"Yep. I'm pretty good at being a go-between for the way it is and the way people will best understand it."

"What's the difference?"

"Exactly."

My phone screen lights up with a text. "Care to use your skills now? It's from my mom."

He holds up a weary hand. "Even I know my limits."

I punch the button.

MY PLANE GETS IN TOMORROW AT 4:07.

I show him the phone. "I cannot believe this. Why? Why now?"

"You really need to ask that?"

"I can't believe this."

"And she's an all-caps person," he observes.

"There's that."

"So, we've got the whole family," he says.

"She's seen all the social media."

He nods. "Must be pretty favorable if she's hopping on the bandwagon."

"It's a little too late."

"Bandwagon's full?"

"Exactly."

The bandwagon is most definitely full.

Jack decides that he's eaten out more than his fair share lately. "I'm going over to the Market and just buy some regular old food."

"What's that?" asks Brandon, coming out on the deck and

looking dumpier than I've ever seen him in old running shorts and another ratty T-shirt.

"Meat loaf, mashed potatoes, peas, and I don't know what for dessert, but definitely something along the order of chocolate."

"Brownies? Pudding?" I ask.

"She loves pudding," Brandon says, pulling over a chair from the table on the other side of the deck.

"Chocolate pudding, then." Jack lifts himself off his lounger, shoves his feet back into his flip-flops.

Wow. We're all wearing green T-shirts. Weird.

After he's gone, Brandon pours himself a tonic and lime and refreshes my drink. We sit inside to watch the news.

"I don't remember you wearing such ratty clothes, Brandon."

"I didn't."

"What changed?"

He shrugs and lifts the hem of the shirt for inspection. Portions of the hem are so frayed it looks as if someone came along and nibbled the fabric like an ear of corn. "When you left, I realized a lot of things. Chiefly, money can't buy happiness. And spending all you have can actually buy the opposite, along with a lot of stuff you don't need."

He clearly has no idea who he's talking to! Maybe showing him the house on Mount Vernon Place isn't such a bad idea at that.

"But you always look nice out there."

"When was the last time you saw me in anything but khakis and a blue blazer? Or my charcoal suit?"

I try to recall the media pictures I've seen of him. "Other than your tux, well, I guess I just don't know."

Crazy.

"But still, you're always jetting off to someplace. With women, usually."

"True. But my trips are always connected to something— an awards show, or some appearance I'm being paid for."

"Really?" I lift my glass to my lips, then lower it again. "I honestly thought you hadn't changed."

"Have you seen my cabin at the ranch recently?"

"Of course not."

He grins his famous, classy bad-boy smile. "Fia, sixteen years is a very long time. A man can come to a lot of realizations and decisions in that space."

"Like what?"

"Like what's really important. After you left us, I realized that what I thought was so great, wasn't. It was that simple. I was a train wreck. You know that."

"Then why did you let me go so easily?"

The words gush out of me and I am horrified. I stand and somehow quickly make my way to the bedroom despite Brandon's calling me to come back and my wound screaming at me just to stop.

I lay myself on the bed and will myself not to cry. But I do anyway, and after all the exertion of the day, I realize as I'm doing so that I am falling asleep, and this makes me happy.

Nineteen

I wake up, check my phone. It's almost 9:00 p.m. Two hours of napping, well, okay. I have two text messages, both from Josia.

Do you need a ride to your appointment tomorrow?

and

How do you feel about bir-
Birch?

I text back immediately.

Yes. It's at 1:30 p.m. And yes. I like birch. How are you?

Good. I'll be by to pick you up at 12:45.

I text him the address and the message that I'll wait out front.

When I make it into the kitchen, Jack is just pulling the meat loaf out of the oven. "Perfect timing! How was your nap?"

"Good."

I face Brandon. "Um, Dad?"

"Let me get you a drink, Fia," Brandon says, his tones bright and filled with earnestness.

"I'm sorry about—"

"No, Fia. Do *not* apologize. You had every right," he says.

"It's true," says Jack, coming to stand by my side.

Brandon must have filled Jack in on my meltdown earlier.

"Thanks. How about some OJ?"

Jack reaches into the refrigerator for the carton of orange juice and hands it to my father.

"Have you heard from Jessica?" I ask.

Brandon sets the glass on the place mat in front of the chair into which I've just lowered myself. He sits down across the table from me. "Yes. I made reservations for her at the Omni."

So she won't be staying here. "That's a relief. Thank you."

"Of course she's upset that I get to stay with you and she doesn't," he says.

"Wonder what social media will say about that?" I take a sip and allow the liquid to sluice away the dry throat my nap left behind.

Brandon nods. "Who cares?"

"Just as long as she doesn't come here," I say.

"I'll try and keep her away," Brandon offers, "so you can just continue to rest, Fia."

"I'll have to see her," I say.

"Then it needs to be on your terms." Jack slices the meat loaf, a ketchup-covered, no-frills meal.

"I'll get her at the airport." Brandon sits down at the kitchen table. "But before that, I have lunch with an old friend from school. He and I reconnected at the luncheon."

"You still all right here on your own, Fia?" Jack asks.

"Yes. Josia is taking me to the follow-up tomorrow afternoon."

"I completely forgot!" Jack says, dropping a liberal amount of butter pats to the mashed potatoes in the stand mixer.

"I can switch my lunch," Brandon offers. "Who's Josia?"

"My boarder."

Brandon's eyes cloud. "You have someone renting out a room? Why?"

"Nothing lasts forever, Brandon. Especially money. You should know that."

❋

Here's what it looks like when your father's heart is breaking in front of you. I'm not foolish enough to believe this is the first time it's broken, but I've never actually witnessed it firsthand. For real, that is.

The proverbial dawn of realization widens his eyes, just a little bit, but as the implications pile up, they widen further, until they snap shut just before his left thumb and middle finger grind the lids against his eyeballs.

This is real.

Fingers remaining in place, he says, "Fia, I am so sorry. I didn't realize. I thought your advisor—"

"No. I lost my shirt when the recession hit. I'm just doing what I need to do to keep my house. I've been saving up Josia's rent money to prepare for a big interview I was going to do up in New York to beat Mother to the punch with her book."

Admiration lights up his eyes. "No kidding!"

Jack looks surprised. "Really?"

I nod. "But that rake decided something else for me. I'm back out in the open now, and there was nothing I could do to stop it or control how it happened."

"How much do you have in your account, Fia?" Dad asks.

"Dad!" I glance over at Jack.

Jack looks shocked. Why? Surely he realized my financial state from our arrangement.

Time to be honest. "A thousand bucks."

My father looks me in the eyes. "It's going to be all right, Fiona."

"I know."

I really do.

❋

I lie on the sofa, belly full of home cooking, looking at the ceiling thinking about all the money I went through, and how much more I could have had. Scripts turned down so I could go on vacation, paid appearances that seemed like too much trouble. Lila and I were even offered our own reality show, but we turned it down. Some things shouldn't be burned into other people's memories.

"It would be the death of your kind of career," she told me when we talked it over. "Mine? Well, it's already not taken seriously."

"But it would give you enough to say good-bye to all of this for good," I said as we hung off the edge of her swimming pool by our calves, our bodies floating in the heated water.

"Love-hate, Fi." She was always talking about the love-hate relationship she had with her dubious fame. "I'm doing all right without that. That's what matters here. Let's not add insult to injury."

"Okay."

"And there's no way I'd let you commit career suicide, Fi. What kind of a friend would I be?"

After that we ordered pizza from Domino's and watched DVDs from her boxed set of *One Day at a Time*.

Lila eventually left Hollywood too. She just did it in a way she'll never get to return if she so chooses. That's the biggest difference between the two of us, and I guess it always was.

Me? I'm stuck here in a world of caught-between. I could go back. I don't want to. But if I wanted to, I could.

I've always known that. I'm the one left to continue an acting family dynasty. I've got connections. I've got clout. I've got opportunity to burn. I'm in a place thousands of actors would kill to be. I am a disgrace to the profession.

But right now my father is playing a game of chess with Jack, and I watch them, concentration on their manly brows, and I see one who has made his fair share of mistakes, and one who hasn't. And my heart is full of affection for both of them.

It's the first time I've ever ridden in Josia's big white pickup truck. The red vinyl seats, carpets, and dash make me feel like I'm sitting inside a warm, friendly heart, and he has some kind of relaxing meditation music rolling through a cassette tape player.

"Doesn't that make you want to go to sleep?" I ask.

"Never."

"Well, that's good."

I catch him up on all the happenings, the impending doom of Jessica's visit, and why the thought of seeing her does that to me.

"I need to ask you," I say, looking out the window on a late-spring Baltimore, my favorite time of year here in this old, lovable town. "Was what I did—the divorce—was it wrong?"

"What do you think?" he asks.

"I'm not sure anymore. At the time, it seemed like the only thing to do."

"Why the doubts? Is it your father being here?"

"Yes."

He stops at a red light and on the corner stands a boy with a window-washing squeegee. Josia points to him and flicks his finger toward himself as if to say, "Come on over."

The youth hurries over, does a horrible job, and Josia gives him a dollar.

"Just a dollar?" the boy says.

"Think about it," Josia says with a laugh. "That took you one minute. You just got paid sixty dollars an hour. Not bad if you ask me, and way more than I make."

The light turns green. He reaches into his pocket and pulls out a business card. "Come see me if you want to make far less doing something far more exhausting, but far more rewarding."

A red Mustang behind us honks. The young man takes the card and we pull away.

"Why did you do that?" I ask.

"Because a few have done well, and one time Avery showed up. Best apprentice I ever had and a truly gifted smith."

"But you're taking such a chance!"

He shakes his head. "Why? I leave it completely up to them if they'd like to come. The people who take me up on it are few and far between. I've been doing this for twenty-seven years, and only ten people have ventured in. It's the opportunity of a lifetime for about a third of them. The rest either don't come back the next day or have quit after about a week. It works out, Fia. It always does."

"It's about finding the people who want a chance."

"Yes, it is. It's like in the coffee shop that day. I knew you needed a chance," he says. "But I also knew that I needed to present it a little differently than usual. I mean, considering what you'd already been through in life."

We pull into the parking lot across the street from the hospital.

"Wait a second." I turn toward him in my seat. "You overheard me in the coffee shop? You weren't my scheduled appointment?"

"Why, no. Did you think I was?"

"Well, yes, I did! The other guy was late, but by the time he got there . . ."

Laughter bends him at the waist. "Well, good! That's very good!"

"Why?" I can't help but begin to join in.

"That means it was just meant to be, Fia. That's all I can say. Would you have entertained the notion otherwise?"

"Of course not."

"Then there you go."

The universe turns large and mysterious all of a sudden, like Someone is secretly seasoning things when no one is looking.

"So back to my question about Dad and the divorce," I prompt him.

"Same thing. Does it matter whether the divorce was right or wrong, when all we're really talking about here and now is giving him another chance? Now you tell me whether *that* is right or wrong."

"It's right."

"As long as *you* say so, Fia."

He pulls into a space and shuts off the truck. "Before I come get you out, may I ask you a question?"

"Yes, of course."

He slides his fingers into his shirt pocket, pulls out a card, then holds it forth in my direction. I stare at it for several seconds before taking it. "It's either you or that boy at the red light for the next apprenticeship."

A squeegee is looking pretty good right now. Wow.

"Hang on, I've got a wheelchair in the back. Believe it or not, I had one hanging around at the forge."

The card stock is smooth and soft, like satin paper. "Just don't bring it home, Josia. I think it's the one thing we *don't* have there."

"Got it."

Written in simple engraved letters, *Josia Yeu, Blacksmith*, the address, and his phone number. That is all.

"Can I think about it?" I ask.

"Of course."

"And if I say no, it won't change what we have now?"

"If you don't know the answer to that, Fia, I'd be shocked."

I laugh. "You're right! Of course it wouldn't change anything. Thank you. Thank you for that."

He snaps open the wheelchair. "Get on in. If you've got to ride in a wheelchair, we'll at least make it fun."

❊

Ten minutes later I'm checking in at the desk. Five minutes after that I'm thinking about "wound care" as I read more information sheets. And really? Wound care? There are doctors who specialize in wounds? It seems like the worst thing to have to deal with. Bodies split open where they shouldn't be, leaving portals to the tender places. It takes a special person to be all about wound care. And the worst wounds seem to involve more senses than should be allowed.

Josia sits down next to me, reaches into his pocket, and pulls out a roll of Lifesavers. I hope the pineapple flavor is on top.

It's not.

"Oh, you get to have the lime!" he says. "That's the best one!"

"Seriously, you can have the lime, Josia. I don't mind."

"No, no, no. I want you to have it, Fia. After all you've been through, you deserve to have the lime."

I pull off the lime and pop it in my mouth.

Maybe lime isn't my favorite normally, but it is right now. This piece of candy tastes better because it's his favorite, freely given, and that's true sweetness.

Is this what Jack was talking about? Receiving love? Could it be so simple as recognizing the beauty in the other's giving?

Let's see.

"Oh, look, Josia. You get the pineapple! That's *my* favorite."

He places the sheer, palest of yellow disc on his tongue and grins. "You know, right now, it's mine too."

Twenty

Well, as they say, nothing good lasts forever. And that's true. Saturn will one day be relegated to something less majestic and funky when the core of our star turns to carbon in an instant and it all goes supernova. So if Saturn has an expiration date, and my lime Lifesaver is no longer on my tongue, I know that these few days of painful bliss, or blissful pain, are about to change into something a little less soft and kind.

The sky is soon to be on fire with the blazing presence of—not Saturn or a supernova, or even a miraculous lime Lifesaver—none other than Jessica Randolph of the Randolphs.

How did everything split wide open so suddenly? First my home, then my leg, and now my heart.

I sit down at the dinette with my father. "So she's going right to the Omni?"

"Yes. I'll head to the airport in a few minutes. I told her you still need another day before you can venture out socially, but we'll have dinner together tomorrow. At least that gives you time to get used to being in the same town." He winks.

"We're going to have to really talk sooner or later, Brandon."

"Yes, Fia. I know that."

"I need more of an explanation than I've had so far."

"Are you sure that's what you want?"

"Positive."

He asks how long until Jack gets home.

"Not until late."

"After I drop your mother off, I'll come right back. I'll bring dinner. If you want the truth, Fia, that's your right."

"I do."

"Jessica's going to have a fit."

"And you're willing to risk that?"

"That's fine. Seriously. All right, I picked up a movie for you this afternoon. Do you want me to set you up on the sofa before I leave?"

"I'd like that."

As I make my way over to the couch a little less slowly than before, he slips in a DVD. "All right, Fia. I'll see you in about two hours."

After arranging my leg on some pillows, I pick up the remote and press Play.

The Little Mermaid. Sweet.

While Ariel goes through the emotional crisis of separating from her loving father—difference number one between Ariel's childhood and mine—I try to replay in my mind what my growing-up years were actually like. Who was my father?

In my mind's eye I see a silhouette against the sliding glass doors leading to the pool. That's the overarching image of patrimony for Fiona Hume. But he's getting more depth now and I like that.

Mother? She's just the same, only a little older looking, and I do mean a little. She's the embodiment of a Twinkie, or that pack of fast food fries you find under the passenger seat of your car three years later, fries that look the same, but . . . really? They can't *be* the same, can they? It's not as if there's some magic realm of suspended animation beneath the passenger seat of your car, as if something's going on there that's simply not visible to the naked eye.

And yet, at least interiorly, Jessica remains the same. By now I can predict her every move, and I know enough to realize she will always be the Me-Me-Me woman she always has been.

But Brandon? Well, he was always nice at least. He may not have been around much, but when he was, he wasn't constantly talking about himself or making me feel bad for "wrecking" his image.

Image.

If there's one thing most people don't quite understand about being an actor, it's this: There's you. And there's Image You. There's who you know yourself to be and who you want others to believe you are.

The healthy players never forget there's a difference between the two.

Was I confusing Brandon's image with Brandon my dad? Was he the one who went through my finances . . . or was it actually Jessica, and he never wanted to impugn her?

Who was really at fault?

And why has it taken me this long to ask these questions?

My cell phone lights up. It's her.

"Hi, Mom."

"Well, I'm here. Where are you? I'm actually hiding in the women's restroom so I'm not bombarded."

Is she kidding me?

"Leg wound?" I ask.

"Oh, come on. So you really are making that bastard pick me up? Do you know it's true? That woman? The divorce? It's not a publicity stunt this time."

"I'm sorry you have to go through this," Robot Fiona says.

"Not sorry enough to arrange proper and fitting transportation, however."

"Where are you?"

"Near baggage claim. And that's another thing. I have to pick up my own bags?"

That's it. "Oh, for hell's sake, Mom! Dad'll be there in a minute. Bugger off! I'll see you tomorrow."

I hang up.

It's a temporary fix, to be sure, but I've never enjoyed delivering a line more.

I turn off the phone because all that incessant ringing from her subsequent calls will drive me insane. Good for me.

❋

When Dad sits down next to me on the couch, he heaves out a sigh.

"She called me," I say. "Sorry."

"Did you really tell her to bugger off? I mean, it doesn't seem like something she'd make up. Jessica's not that creative, but I don't think I've ever heard you—"

"Yes."

"I was hoping you'd say that."

"How is she?"

He reaches next to him for a throw pillow, puts it on the arm of the sofa, and lays out some, his feet still on the floor. "Exactly as you might imagine. I guess all I can do is thank you for taking the heat off of me for a few hours."

I adjust my leg. "Is this the way it's always been? She's treated you like this too? I mean, I kinda guessed it, but I just figured you let it roll off of you, nonstick."

He shakes his head. "I wish that had been possible. The only way I could stand it was to build my own place. She either had to find me, or I could choose to go see her."

"Wow."

"I don't know, Fia. Couples do what they have to do sometimes. A divorce probably should've happened. And it should have been your mother and me; instead, it was you." He shakes his head. "I'm sorry."

I take his hand. "It's never straightforward, is it? I mean, there was a lot going on behind the scenes with me. Stuff, well, Mom knew, I'm pretty sure. But I've never talked with you about Campbell. I don't know if you even know. I always figured you did, but never knew for sure."

He squeezes my fingers. "I knew. I didn't want to bring it up in case it would damage you even further. Nobody tells us what to do in these situations, Fia. Your mother said she'd be there for you through it, and I just did my part by handling it with Campbell."

"What?" His part with Campbell? "I have no idea what you mean."

"You said you wanted the truth?"

"I do."

"Then here goes. And for what it's worth, Fia, I wish I had gone with my instinct then and told your mother I wanted to be there for you in a way you actually knew about."

I hold up a hand. "No, Dad. Don't. Believe me, I can hear

her, talking about how this is a girl thing, how she'll take one for the team and bear the emotional brunt of it so you don't have to. All that self-sacrificial drama that makes her seem like the savior of the world, when really, it's about her racking up points on her side, keeping herself in the martyr's chamber. Believe me, I wasn't fooled then, and I'm not fooled now. You, however. I never knew what to think."

"I wasn't around enough."

"There's that. Anyway, tell me about Campbell."

"Of course you remember *Galaxy Goons*, right?"

I nod.

"Okay. When your mother and I became aware that Campbell was abusing you, she, of course, was frightened for your career—"

"*Her* career."

"Well, yes, but I always try to give her the benefit of the doubt when I can."

"She relies on that."

He continues, "And she wanted to just pretend that nothing was going on."

"That's what happened for a couple of months."

"Right. Until I found out about it. I met with Campbell and, God's honest truth, Fia, I wanted to kill him. I came up with the most horrifying, grandiose schemes in my head, ideas that would put Wes Craven in a mental institution."

"Good." I really mean that. I needed somebody to *want* to kill him, even if they didn't do it.

His words, though violent around the edges, are inflated by love. "It taught me to hate, Fia. For the first time in my life I hated with something so pure inside me." He grabs my other hand too. "I didn't realize it. I didn't realize something so dark could be so unadulterated."

"Nobody tells you that. You just can't know until you feel it."

"You think you know . . ."

"But you don't. Not unless someone like Campbell comes along. I'm glad you hate him too."

"Oh, after what you went through because of him? I'll hate him forever and be glad to do it."

We smile at each other. Not the smile of a shared sentiment, but the smile of knowing someone else is as raw inside as you are, the smile of realizing, for the first time, you're not alone in this.

And I never was. I just thought I was. "Go on, Dad."

"Your contract was ironclad, and for me to tell the world about what a low-life, scumbag child molester he was would end your career for good—I didn't really care about your mother's, or my own, for that matter. If I went the legal route, it would be your word against his, and his legal machine against mine. Because I had wasted most of our money, our legal machine would have been like a calculator going up against a super-computer to get you out of that contract."

"So he had your ass in a wringer."

"Yes."

"Damn it! I hate that! I hate that so much!"

I feel the helpless waves of castrated anger crash over me and fill me afresh, that feeling I'd been trying to avoid, that helplessness, that helplessness.

He sits up straight, scoots right next to me, and embraces me. "I'm sorry, Fia."

"I rarely hope hell is real, Dad. But sometimes, just for people like Campbell, I hope it is. I really hope it is."

What Brandon doesn't know is how much it happened. How my early calls weren't because my hair and makeup took that long. It was a teen show, for hell's sake. No, the driver would drop me off at an empty building.

And Campbell always had music playing. Always a different kind, as if he wanted to taint everything for the foreseeable future. I hate it all.

His office was purple. *Purple!* The man ruined purple for me!

His fingers. Inside me. His horrid mouth with the slobbery tongue. That hairy belly. Everything. Just everything about him deserves a bath in acid.

"What is it about the world?" I ask. "Why do the predators have so many advantages? I hate that."

"Me too," he whispers.

"Can you get me some OJ?" I ask.

"Yes," he says, a little relief in his tone.

❀

Brandon hands me my juice and sits down. I take a sip. "So what happened when you met with Campbell?"

His actions mirror my own as he readies himself to speak. He sets his glass down on the end table next to him. "He was livid with the confrontation, to be sure. I told him he couldn't have you anymore. The show had to be over. Of course he threatened to sue me for everything we had. But I had a trump card." He pauses.

"Which was?"

"Me."

"Oh no." It's all clear. *Galaxy Goons.*

"Yes."

"You agreed to sabotage your career to get me out of there?"

"What else could I do, Fia?"

He doesn't crumble into tears, and surely a different kind of man would have just beaten the crap out of Campbell and said, "I'll see you in court, you bastard."

But that isn't my dad. He doesn't have that sort of machismo residing inside of him. And that's not always bad. Instead, he laid himself on the altar.

"The crazy thing is," he continues, *"Galaxy Goons* was an instant hit, and I've had to talk about it ever since. But for me, the project—"

"And here I always thought you didn't want to talk about it because it was such a departure. So goofy compared to all your serious roles."

He gathers me to himself. "No. It was because every time I thought about it, or talked about it, I remembered what that man did to my daughter."

"Why didn't you tell me?"

"Your mother—"

"Thought it best I didn't have to bear that kind of burden. Is that right?"

"Yes. And I agreed with her. People take things on themselves, making it their own fault, when they shouldn't."

Brandon wasn't malicious. He was just weak when it came to his wife. An age-old tale with the strongest of men. And not completely weak at that. He simply used the most valuable bargaining chip he possessed and gained by negotiation what a lot of men would have taken by force.

"Dad?" I ask. "If you could do it all over again, how would you do it differently?"

His arms tighten around me. "I would have stood my ground in what I believed then, and what I still believe to this day. You being an actor was a choice you alone should have made, even if you had never done so. That would have been all right with me."

"But my mother was a Randolph. And Randolph children—"

"'Always make the best actors.'" We finish Jessica's quote together.

He pulls back and searches my face. "Fia, honey. You can be whoever you want to be. I want to tell you that right now. I should have told you that when you went off to film your first commercial when you were four years old. Your life and what you want to do with it is yours to decide, and yours alone. And what is more, I will support you, be by your side, and cheer you on with whatever you decide, even if it changes from one day to the next. I love you, baby. I always have. I'll spend the rest of our time here on earth together proving every single word of what I just said. And nobody will ever tell me otherwise."

I rest my forehead against his chest and I cry. Weeping in the simple light of being seen by my father for the very first time.

Twenty-One

He said to call anytime if I needed him. Isn't that right? I hope he meant it. People say a lot of things without truly thinking about timing.

But really, Josia did say to call whenever.

I rest my fingertips on the smooth front of my phone and slide it off the nightstand toward me.

Three seconds later his phone is ringing. Two seconds after that, the words, "Fia, are you okay?" seem to drip like honey down from the heavens.

Seriously. It sounds that good.

"Can you come pick me up? I want to come home, Josia. Just for a little bit."

"I'm on my way. Be there in ten."

"Are you sure?"

"It's good, Fia. See you soon."

He didn't sound at all groggy, I think as I slip into my

sweatpants and one of Jack's Notre Dame sweatshirts. I can't find my beastly sweater anywhere, and I have to admit, if Jack burned it behind my back, I not only wouldn't blame him, I'd be thankful.

I'm happy to report to myself that getting dressed took half the time it did when I first came home from the hospital, and that I truly am on the mend.

When Josia pulls the truck up exactly ten minutes after our conversation, I'm stepping off the last stair. He swings open his door and rushes toward me.

I have to admit it. I've overtaxed myself. I stop and steady my hand against the handrail. "Wow," I whisper. Some real pain meds would be good right about now.

"You okay?" he says, now at my side.

I nod. "I think so. I was feeling better than I had been up there, but now . . ."

"Too much, too soon." He bends at the waist and picks me up in his arms, gently accounting for my leg. "Let's get you to the truck."

You read in books how a man will pick up a woman like she "weighs almost nothing." So, okay, that's not exactly the case with Josia. He's not a large man. But he's strong and he carries me with ease. In fact, speaking as someone who has been picked up like this a lot of times, particularly during my teen romance comedy phase that lasted about five films, I feel the most supported this time.

His shirt feels soft and worn under my fingers and along the length of my arm. But the freshly laundered smell reaches my nostrils as I lay my head against his chest. The warmth of him infuses into me and I'm ready, it seems. Ready for what?

Well, to get in the truck at the very least.

I laugh. Just a little.

"What is it?" he asks, gently depositing me on the red vinyl seat.

"I'm happy," I say.

It isn't an overwhelming euphoria as if I'm tripping without the necessary substances. It just simply is.

"Good."

He swings around to his side, hops in, then pulls us away from the house and into the night streets of a city sleeping beneath a clear sky and a sweet breeze coming down off the mountains a hundred miles away. Or maybe a thousand miles. Maybe a million. It doesn't matter, does it?

"It's a beautiful night, isn't it?" I ask, thinking I should put the seat belt on, but knowing I'm safe.

He looks over at me and smiles the widest grin I've seen on him to date. "It's all beautiful," he says. "Every bit of it, yes?"

❋

He lets us in the front door of the house, then flips on the light. I gasp. He's cleared the entry hall of its clutter, swept it clean, and replaced every single light in the chandelier. The sparkling, winking chandelier is now burning bright, throwing a pure and white light around the white room, bouncing it off the marble floors in a way that speaks of a healing sun.

"Josia!"

"Welcome home, Fia. I hope you don't mind. It's the only place I took the liberty to work on without your permission, but only because I was positive this was what you'd want."

"It is!"

"And I wanted you to have a proper homecoming."

I turn to him and hug him, his blacksmith arms coming around to hold me tightly. So much comfort here.

What is Josia to me? A friend? A father? A brother? The one who will always be there no matter what?

Yes, yes, yes, to all of these.

"I don't understand," I whisper. "How can this even be?"

"I don't sleep much, if you want to know the truth."

I laugh. Let him answer the wrong question. It's okay.

"And when you don't sleep," he continues, "you can be there for people in a way others can't."

Oh, so he did understand.

I pull away from him. "So where to next? I have a feeling this isn't it."

"Oh, heavens, no! Come on back to the kitchen." He pockets his keys, curves his arm through mine, and we proceed down the hallway—the hallway I've walked down so many times without thinking about it, the hallway that was dreary and sometimes dank, the hallway that led to more piles of wasted thoughts and maladjusted intentions now unrolled before my feet with more anticipation than any red carpet could previously hope to have afforded.

"They say the kitchen is the heartbeat of a home," Josia says, stopping three feet shy of the doorway. "Close your eyes, Fia, if you don't mind."

I don't. So I do.

He gently steps with me, leading me to the threshold. "Good. Open your eyes."

Twenty-Two

I remember when I was a younger woman shooting a picture in England about a family that set out to the East Indies when their son was falsely accused of murder. They left under the cover of night from Dover, and there we filmed the scenes, the chalky white cliffs every bit as inspiring as I had imagined ahead of time.

On a day my name failed to appear on the shooting schedule, I sauntered over to Canterbury to take stock of the town, a place so old that nails holding some of the buildings together were in place well before my mother's family came to America. And they came over on the *Mayflower*.

I kid you not.

I wandered the narrow, cobbled streets of the town, stopping for lunch in a little place that looked as if it hadn't changed since the days of Queen Elizabeth I. I ordered what the menu described as cheesy biscuits, whereupon I received six little diamond-shaped cheese crackers on a plate. I don't think I've ever been more disappointed in my life.

Having expected a fuller tummy, I set back out into the street still yearning for biscuits dripping with butter and melted cheese, and before long came upon the cathedral. Canterbury Cathedral, where Archbishop Thomas à Becket was murdered by the machinations of Henry the VIII.

What I didn't expect walking into the great stone building was the fullness of the knowledge that I had wandered into the most beautiful building I had ever been in, or ever would be in.

Sometimes you just know.

And I know now, without a doubt, that I am in the most beautiful room I will ever inhabit for my own.

As white and colorless as the entry hall is, this room is equally as colorful and warm. And alive!

Handmade cabinet fronts in warm woods gleam with a satiny finish.

"The crib ends!" he says, and I clap.

The countertops covered in mosaics depict space and planets and earth and nature. All four corners of the globe. All of space and time, it seems.

"I've never seen anything more beautiful in my life," I marvel.

"I used the tile you've collected. And my goodness! You arranged things according to color in each room? That made things so much easier, so thank you."

I gaze at him, incredulity taking two of its fingers and prying open my mouth.

"And it only gets better from here, Fia," he says. "I've got plans and I hope you'll help me."

I remember the card he handed me, reach down into my purse, and pull it out. "Will you show me how to be a blacksmith too?"

His eyes sparkle. "I can't think of anything I'd like more. Let's sit down and get the weight off that leg."

Between the two windows looking out over the backyard, a small table forged of black iron with three matching chairs rests on the kitchen floor, once a battered linoleum, now painted wood. A candle burns in the center of an iron medallion depicting the sun and moon, matching the sun he made for me weeks earlier. "And you'll teach me how to make chairs and tables and lawn ornaments?"

"Of course. Whatever your head can dream up and my skills can help you achieve, we'll do together."

"How about a cup of tea?" I ask, gesturing toward one of the chairs. "Have a seat."

He smiles, and a look of satisfaction travels from the edges of his mouth up to the corners of his eyes and fills them with happiness.

We sit together, drinking tea and saying little as we watch the sun rise outside the windows, healing a garden I've left for far too long, a garden I want to make beautiful with every piece of my heart.

"One more surprise," he says. "Hang on."

I swear the man must be able to suspend time. How can a person get so much done in just a few days?

He returns from his bedroom with a pristine ivory coat hanging from his fingers by the collar. "I repaired this for you. I hope you don't mind. I found it crumpled on the floor when I went down in the basement to see if there was any paint down there I could use for the floor. And then I saw the buttons on the table there, put two and two together—"

I can't believe my eyes. "Lila's coat," I whisper, gently taking it from his grasp.

"I had to modify it a little bit. I wanted to use the buttons exactly like you left them on the bench. Now, if you don't like what—"

"I love it!" I stand up and hold the garment to my heart. "I love it so much!"

The tears fall, and he puts his arms around me and holds me close.

"I love you, Fia," he says. "You are wonderful."

"Just as I am?" I ask, looking up to search his eyes.

"Just as you are. Every single day."

❀

He drops me off back at Jack's just before six thirty, gives me a little hug at the door, and says to call him anytime. It really is fine and he enjoyed my company.

I'm glad I took him at his word.

"When do you think you'll be coming back home?" he asks. "And is there anything else you want me to do?"

"I'll be back when Jessica heads back to Idaho. I don't want her even tempted to see my house. I don't know why this is, Josia, but right now I just can't."

"It's okay, Fia. Well, I guess I'll make an early morning of it at the forge. Call me if you need me."

As I tread the stairs to the stoop, Josia climbs into his truck, waiting until I shove my key in the lock and the door opens beneath my push. He pulls away.

Actually, I *do* know why I don't want Jessica at my house. I don't want her brand of acid drizzling down over all that is beautiful, eating away at my progress and my hope for the future until it resembles what she is comfortable with, what she can control, what she can use to further herself.

But she's still my mother, right?

Or is she? Is that what mothers do, rip away any kind of security you have, undermine any personal growth unless it's to further their own self-image? No, thanks.

But when I think of everything she's done for me . . .

Wait. That's it exactly.

Think and remember, Fia. Remember *every* little thing.

I shut the front door and lean against it to rest for a second. My leg feels better than it has so far, and though it is still painful, the stiffness has lessened.

Jack's asleep on the couch. "Jack," I whisper, tapping him on the shoulder.

His eyes open and right away he smiles. "Fi? You're already up? Are you okay?"

"I'm better than ever. I want you to get ready and take me over to my mom's hotel."

He sits up immediately. "Really? Right now, as in, right now?"

"Uh-huh. No better time than the present."

"What's going on?" He swings his feet to the floor and stands. "Do you want breakfast first?"

"I'll make it."

"Are you sure you can handle standing that long?"

"I'll soon find out."

He heads toward his bedroom and calls over his shoulder, "I think you can do whatever you set your mind to, Fia."

And in that moment, I realize that I love him.

❀

Brandon, however, isn't as optimistic. Then again, he knows Jessica far better than Jack does. "Are you sure you don't want me to go with you? I've got the rental car."

He's setting the breakfast table as I scramble eggs. The coffee-maker is sputtering and I'm ready for the first sip. And the second and the third.

"I'm sure, Dad. Really. I have to do this on my own."

"I know." He reaches into the silverware drawer for forks. "I just know how she can be."

"Better than anyone," I admit. "But honestly, this isn't about anything other than my relationship with her. It's not your problem anymore, Dad."

He side-hugs me. "I'm proud of you."

Jack stands at the doorway. "This might be one of the hardest things you've ever done."

"I know." I tip the skillet over a bowl and slide the eggs in with the spatula. "But it's time."

Talk about a divorce.

Is this right? Am I really supposed to do this to my own parent?

And she might come around, admit she's been a selfish person all these years, admit her failings as a parent, and we go on from there.

I'll give her that chance.

But this is it. No more chances, no more catty calls and manipulating me with her emotional ploys. I'm done. If I don't do it now, I'll hate her for the rest of my life.

Twenty-Three

I text Jessica, arranging to meet her in the lobby at noon. We can catch a cab and go over to Little Italy for lunch. My dad's family has always preferred Chiapparelli's, and although Jessica usually prefers the more "it" places, I'm not taking no for an answer.

She agrees by saying, *I hate that place, but it will be worth it if I can see you, darling.*

I show Jack the phone. He rolls his eyes. "Sometimes there are no words for how gullible people think a person can be," he says.

"I need you to do me a favor," I ask. "Can you drive me to the Galleria, get me there by ten so I can do some shopping? I want to look absolutely amazing."

Deborah Raines be damned. I'll spend that money and be glad to do so.

He reaches across the breakfast table, grabs my arm, and

squeezes. "Of course I will. I'll get a little work in beforehand and we'll leave here at nine forty-five."

I head into the living room where Dad watches the morning news show hosts dance the fine line between journalism and entertainment.

"Dad," I say. "I'm going shopping. I want to look really great when I meet Jessica for lunch."

He sets the remote on the coffee table. "How about a daddy-daughter shopping spree? We've never had one of those, and I'd say we're long overdue."

I grin, catching a dim reflection of myself in the sliding glass doors, wondering at that ghost of a girl in front of my eyes, the girl who looks so much like I used to feel, the girl who's quickly fading to nothing. And good riddance.

❋

After shopping with my father, getting photo after photo snapped by onlookers, I'm sitting in the hotel bar, absolutely exhausted but looking good in a flirty yellow floral sundress and flat, red sandals. I found the dress right away, on sale, despite all the gawkers. Dad and I put on a nice little show, and I still had time for a blowout. My now-flowing hair looks decently fluffy in all the right places.

But the best thing? It turned a little chilly, and around my shoulders, Lila's coat gives me strength.

Sipping on a lemonade, I compose myself, thankful I had the foresight to get dressed up for this. In entertainment terms, I'm armed and dangerous because, facts are facts: I'm young and pretty, and Jessica isn't young. She's far prettier, yes. But that doesn't matter. Her beauty is attained and maintained, and everyone seems to want what they cannot have. Poor Jessica will nevermore possess a youth that doesn't come from being able to afford it. Much like a house or a garden, without maintenance, and a lot of it, it will fade like the paint on my porch pillars.

In her own terms, I win. In fact, given a youth culture like we've got, I've already won.

And a part of my heart goes out to her. This is the battlefield of Jessica Randolph.

It isn't fair. It's absolutely meaningless to have some sort of competition set up in the first place over something that simply is or isn't.

I'm old. You're young.

I'm young. You're old.

Who the hell cares?

But right now I need this to feel strong.

And, Mom, if you weren't so worried about being young, you could have been the coolest older lady ever. If you wanted to be in competition so damned bad, why not make yourself even cooler than Jessica Tandy was? Why put yourself at odds with women possessing half the wisdom and life experience you might have built up to become amazing?

In this moment, my head-space filled with the same old monkey chatter that has cluttered it for years, I actually listen to myself take stock of my own advice. The woman who has tormented me for as long as I can remember has to go. And the woman I've used inside my head to torment myself? She has to go too.

❊

There she is.

I watch her walk away from the bank of elevators, enter the lobby proper, and look around as if she's looking for me when I know full well she's looking to see who is looking at her, and, might I add, she's looking as stunning as ever.

But I can x-ray right through those summer white pants and the nautical shirt with the Hermès scarf tied around her blond hair. The gold jewelry and perfect, patent leather flats don't fool me at all.

She wants worship, and she wants it right now.

I look down at my lemonade, pretending to be absorbed in my own thoughts, unaware of the show in front of me. If all the world's a stage, my mom wrote the manual on how to block it perfectly to suit any production and venue.

She makes her way up to me, taps me on the shoulder playfully, and smiles, eyes lifting to the bartender almost imperceptibly. "Hey, you," she says, as if we saw each other for the last time yesterday, not more than ten years ago.

"Hi, Jessica." I'm striving for pleasant but not overly emotional, and definitely not needy. "Have a seat."

"Drinks first?" She slides onto the stool and sets her electric-blue designer tote in her lap. One smile at the bartender brings him right over. "Lemonade for me as well, please. Diet, if you have it."

The way she nods him off probably makes him feel as if he has been given the quest of a lifetime. Sir Galahad of the bubbler machine. It amazes me how this works with other people but fails to have an effect on me.

"Shall I call a cab?" she asks.

Time in a cab with Jessica? Trapped in a moving vehicle? Little Italy will have to wait for another day. "No. Let's have lunch here. My leg is tired after the morning with Dad."

Her eyebrow rises at my use of his title, not his name, but she says nothing.

"I thought it would be good to walk around a little this morning and he did too," I explain.

Her lips purse in a pouty way. "Well, I would think it's a little too soon, but never mind about that."

This from the woman who wanted me to pick her up at the airport yesterday afternoon.

The bartender arrives with her drink. "Menus?" she asks.

"Right away," he says. I judge Lyle (according to his name tag) to be in his midthirties, a gym rat when he's not plying the trade of cocktails, maybe a little difficult to deal with if you're in a relationship with him and you're not as good-looking as he is, but otherwise generally harmless.

Ten seconds later we're looking at the usual "pub fare" menu large hotels sometimes have in their Irish pubs that are anything but. I don't have to look twice. If the menu says "fish and chips" somewhere, my decision was made the day it rolled off the printing press.

After we order, Jessica requesting the Cobb salad, light on the blue cheese and the bacon (some mysteries cannot be explained), she takes a sip of her lemonade. "Fish and chips? Really, Fiona?"

"Look at me."

"Bad for your heart. Some people can be skinny as rails and still have fat around their organs and clogging up their veins."

"I'm thirty-two."

"Still and all."

The question is, do I strike at the beginning of all this, or ease into it?

My phone lights up with a text from Dad: *I'll pick you two up at two. Studio tour all set. They're looking forward to it. I think you'll be pleasantly surprised.*

"Who was that from?" Jessica asks.

"Dad."

"What's this 'Dad' business? Since when did you start calling him Dad?"

"Since we had one of those conversations we should have had years ago."

Her eyes cloud momentarily and I can hear the electricity-speed thoughts. *What did they talk about? Was it about my career? Her career? Surely it wasn't about Campbell. I did the right thing. Was it about Brandon's new girlfriend? Was it about assets? Maybe my new movie? Have they seen it somehow? Did they hate it?*

"Well, good. Let that stay between you two. I'm happy for you both."

She turns her stool away from me a few inches and lays both hands on the bar. "I don't suppose you've heard about what happened with me yesterday. Of course not. Not with your leg and all, but anyway."

"No, I haven't."

"Well, it appears that my tweets about you caught the attention of Deborah Raines, and she wants me to come on her show and talk about motherhood. She said it was all so touching and the world needs to see and hear from a dedicated parent like me."

Thank God I didn't have anything in my mouth or Lyle would have had to administer the Heimlich maneuver. The type of acting that got me an Oscar shows up, and thank God for it. "Wow," I say. "Pretty crazy, huh?"

"Isn't that amazing? The show called this morning. Of course I said I would. It's a chance to even up the score."

"Well, good for you," I say, drawing her in, needing to hear her egocentric babbling in all its glory for the final time. "When do you fly to New York?"

"This evening, actually. I just got word. I only have time for lunch and then I have to get an outfit to appear on camera tomorrow."

"So, no go on the *Charm City Killings* set visit with Deborah Raines waiting in the wings?" I ask.

"Hardly. It's like you said. That show isn't what it used to be. I'd be stooping." She leans forward and sips her diet lemonade.

"Did you tell her why you came to Baltimore?"

"Of course. They were so impressed and promised me I'd be on the first flight back here tomorrow. I told them you're an adult, of course, and doing well, but I couldn't stay away for long."

Not to mention I've already been in this state for days.

Another text from Dad comes through: *You surviving?*

I chuckle and I see so much of what was hidden before the rusty old rake pulled the blindfold away from my vision.

It's time. Time to let go of this person who was supposed to protect me, guide me, and love me when it didn't always suit her. That's not the way I want to live my life anymore. Wondering why I wasn't enough, why she cared more about herself.

"Well, fish and chips or not, I'm done." I stand up, and although my leg is on fire, I don't wince or cry out. I summon all my skills.

"What are you talking about? What are you doing?" she asks, panic suddenly flitting across her perfect face.

"I'm leaving, Mother. And you can't come with me anymore."

The corners of her mouth turn down. "You're not making any sense, Fiona. Now sit down and stop risking a scene."

I used to be very good at scenes.

"No, Jessica. I'm telling you what's going to happen this time because I know you well enough to know how you're going to respond. I'm going to walk across this bar, out into the lobby, and onto the street. And you will not follow me. You won't follow me any longer.

"And what's more, I'm going to get in a cab and go back to my friend Jack's house, collect my things, and go home. Home-home, to my big, achy, old house that needs a lot of work, but so much has been done. And it's beautiful underneath it all. It's simply the most beautiful place ever."

She reddens and opens her mouth.

"No. Don't speak. After that, Dad is going to take me over to Jasper Venn's studio and I'm going to tour it, without you, because I've thought about it, and maybe a little guest spot, doing what I'm good at, being the best actor the Randolph family has ever seen—and yes, I believe that—would be just right. And I'll come home to work on my beautiful house with my beautiful friends, and learn to become a blacksmith and make an archway for my weird friend at the coffee shop. Sometimes I'll ride my bike to Fort McHenry and watch the sun on the water and my life will truly be a thing of beauty. In fact, it already is."

"You're speaking nonsense, Fiona." Her mouth has slimmed in rage. "Stop this right now!" she hisses.

"I'm done already. If I thought anything you ever did was truly for me, I'd feel guilty about this, but I don't. You threw me to that wolf Campbell again and again, and someday I may have the strength to forgive you for that, but today I only have it in me to make sure you never, ever hurt me again. I only have the strength to walk away and not look back."

In a movie script, I might lean down and give her a hug, change up the mood for just a second so the audience knows there's still hope. But this is my life, and as far as my mother is concerned, there is none.

I turn and walk away knowing without a doubt she will let me go.

Twenty-Four

Jasper Venn's assistant, a man in his late twenties named Shane, greets us in the lobby of the production facility.

"I remember this place," Dad says, looking around him inside the entry of what was once a Catholic grade school in Highlandtown. "We used to come here for sour beef and dumplings every fall."

"They just stopped doing that a few years ago. Shame," the assistant says, looking hip in grass-green skinny pants and an old-man beard. "Did you ever try the fried oysters?"

Dad nods. "Oh yes."

"I had no idea you were from Baltimore. You seem more international." Shane points up the cement staircase. "Offices are on the second floor."

"Do you do a lot of the shooting in the basement?" I ask, not a stranger to the fund-raising dinners the parish, Sacred Heart of Jesus, threw every fall.

"You got it." He follows us up the staircase. "Take a right down the hallway. Can I get you a beverage?"

"I'm fine," I say.

"I wouldn't mind a cup of coffee," Dad says.

"You got it." Shane directs us into a room obviously once a classroom but now a lounge. I like the vibe, clean and modern with some sheik's tent mixed in to make it comfortable and warm.

I sit down on a turquoise-and-ivory houndstooth sofa. Dad stands beside me in front of a coffee table surfaced with old license plates holding up several large photography books. "This is nice," I say.

Shane checks his buzzing phone. "I'll get that coffee and tell Jasper you're here. Just sit tight and I'll be right back."

"You got it," says Dad.

I stifle a laugh as Shane leaves the room. "You do seem international."

Dad shakes his head. "Nobody realizes that at least fifty percent of my life is spent in ratty T-shirts and cargo shorts."

"I didn't even realize it!"

"Isn't that a shame?"

I could be sad about that, but I feel free after my conversation with Jessica to feel whatever comes naturally. "Well, we'll just have to make up for lost time."

Man, I come up with the cheesiest dialogue on my own. It's a good thing I'm an actor, not a writer.

"I'm counting on that, Fia."

Well, at least Brandon's not any better at it. Like father, like daughter.

Jasper Venn strides into the room, his hair in its feathery gray glory, a warm, wonderful mane around his face. "When Shane told me about your call, I couldn't believe it. Absolutely could not. Welcome to Charm City Radio Pictures, Mr. Hume, and Ms. Hume."

So this is what it feels like to be by your father's side as people who ply the same trade?

I place my hand in Jasper's and we shake. "Thanks for having us in at such short notice."

"I'm just in town for a couple of days," Dad explains. "But I've heard good things about your studio and wanted to peek my head in."

"Always welcome," Jasper says as Shane enters with a mug of coffee.

He hands it to Dad. "Black?" he asks.

"You got it," Dad says, taking the cup, and I want to laugh this time too.

Jasper gestures toward the door. "Would you like a tour?"

I start to nod, but Dad holds up his hand. "That won't be necessary. I'll cut straight to the chase, Jasper. Your show isn't doing too well, and it seems to me that it isn't because the quality is going down. I think you were on the front of the wave of good TV, and by raising the standards you created a wealth of competition."

He's good.

Everybody sits down, Dad and I on the sofa, Jasper on the club chair.

"I couldn't have said it better myself," Jasper says, crossing one leg over the other.

Dad raises a finger. "I have an idea that might be of some help."

"Would you like to guest direct?" Jasper asks.

Dad smiles. "As much of an honor as that would be, thank you, no. I'm thinking about something else."

This is going to be good. I have no idea what he's thinking.

"All right." Jasper leans forward a little.

"I'm not sure if you were aware of the fact that my daughter here lives in Baltimore."

"I wasn't until very recently." He gestures toward my leg. "I would have offered you a guest spot on the show."

I hold up my hand. "I'm not acting anymore, but thank you." No sense in showing my hand when I don't even know what cards I've got.

"I'd like to relocate," Dad says with no warning whatsoever. None.

"What? Dad, no! You've got—"

"What? All the bloody crap out there?" He turns back to Jasper. "Pardon my language."

Jasper laughs. "You don't have to tell me! I'm already here, aren't I?"

I straighten in my seat.

"So I'm not asking for a guest director spot. I want to know if you'd like Brandon Hume to breathe new life into your show."

"But, Dad, you've never done television."

"It's good television," says Dad. "And I'm getting too old for motion pictures. It's much too grueling. It's time for me to settle down into a more scheduled, disciplined life. It's time to learn how to do that."

Jasper holds up a hand. "Don't get me too excited, now. We're on a fixed income." He laughs.

"We can come up with something, I'm sure." Dad turns to me. "What do you think, Fia? Me moving to Baltimore?"

"I think it would be great."

"And maybe a guest spot or two for you, Fia?" Jasper asks.

I shrug and wrinkle my nose. "We'll see."

"What are you doing right now?" Jasper asks my dad.

"This is what's on my schedule for today."

"Well then, let's talk further. Do you want to come to my office for a bit?" Jasper stands.

"I would."

"And I'll give you both the grand tour."

I stand too. "As for me, I think I'm going to head back home. Home-home," I say to Dad. "Why don't you and Jack come over for dinner later on? I'll give him a call. Is seven good?"

"I'll be there."

I kiss him on the cheek. "I'll see you then."

I just invited my father over for dinner like it was the most normal thing in the world.

❋

Jasper offered up Shane to drive me. In the car, I call Tony to arrange for the exclusive interview and photo shoot we had discussed. "I've got a story to tell, Tony. It isn't pretty, but it explains a lot."

"You just tell me when and where, Fiona," he says. "And we'll make it happen."

So that's in the works. Good.

When we arrive at my first stop, the Bizarre, I thank Shane for the lift and head into the shop.

True to form, Randi stands behind the counter with her Sudoku book. She looks up at the clanging of the bells on the glass door. "Fiona!"

For the first time that I've ever seen, she runs out from behind the counter, slamming the game book down as she does so. The pencil goes flying across the floor toward the table of old men, but she pays it no attention. And now I'm in her big-lady arms, and she smells like coffee beans and brown sugar and roses.

"You had me worried sick!" she says as she pulls back to take a look at me. "How's the leg? I didn't believe a word Perez said about you, other than you were injured. Where have you been? Who's been taking care of you? Other than your dad, but I assume that's been a big publicity stunt. And your mother, dear Lord in heaven, she's been a piece of work on Twitter!" She comes up for air and I strike.

"Brandon has been amazing! Jessica got the boot. Josia redid my kitchen, and I think I'm finally able to love a man."

Yes, yes, yes. This is all true. So much so that the simplicity of the words feels about as right as a sunrise over mountains or the gasp of knowing that occurs when you realize for the first time that you understood something you'd been trying to grasp for years, and the difficulty wasn't in its complexity but its simplicity. There was something you'd been missing, something you didn't even know to look for.

Yes, yes. This is my life now.

This is my life now.

"Wow! Well, sit down at the counter and let me make you a congratulatory latte."

She gets to work and I fill her in on what's transpired over the course of mere days, but I have to check my own thoughts. A lot of groundwork was laid, as if an unseen hand was preparing me for today, even down to the scraping of a rusty rake over my thigh.

After the latte has been consumed and Randi's curiosity is appeased, I bring up the topic of the doorway arch.

"Oh yeah?" asks Randi. "Any ideas?"

"I'm about to head down to Josia's forge. He doesn't realize I'm coming."

"I have to admit I had my doubts about him, Fiona, but he's been a super-good friend."

"I know. Good things happen in your shop, Randi. I hope you know that." I smile. I'm giddy. I haven't felt this much hope in years, if ever, really.

Okay, yes, really. Never before.

What a day.

"He said he'd teach me how to weld. And so, well, I've collected a lot of junk here and there, you know."

"Yes, I do." She starts wiping down the counter. "But only because you've said so."

"A lot of it is stuff I can weld together. And then maybe paint it all. What color? What color would you like, Randi? I'm thinking red, or orange, something warm, you know?"

Oh my gosh, I'm talking like an artist, and I have no idea if I can even do the job.

I can. Not because I have to, but because if I don't, I'll be shortchanging the miracles that have been exploding like fireworks around me all of my life.

They do that, you know. Miracles do. Even in the rainiest of seasons, they break through with their sparks of light and life. You just have to make up your mind not to concentrate on the rain.

I wanted it to be otherwise. I wanted the good in life to be so centered in front of my face I couldn't help but be happy. I wanted joy to be delivered like a surprise bouquet of flowers and yet taken for granted at the same time.

And maybe that's exactly how it works. Nobody told me, however, that when joy comes knocking, you simply have to open the door, look it in the eye with hope, not doubt, expectation, not fear, and give it permission to come right in.

It's up to me. It always has been. And instead of chastising myself that I didn't realize it for so long, I raise my eyes in thankfulness that I uncovered this when I did.

I'm only thirty-two years old.

My entire life stands before me, and for the first time ever, I'm not looking behind me.

Note from the Author

I have suspended the laws
of kitchen renovation to suit my purposes.

Reading Group Guide

1. Although *A Thing of Beauty* isn't meant to be read as an allegory, who or what does Josia represent for you?

2. What is the difference between running away from our circumstances and reinventing ourselves or our lifestyles? How do we know if our choices denote healthy change or a refusal to address the past?

3. What does Fia's house mean to her, and to you?

4. How do you think you would fare living out your life under a microscope, whether it's of your own choosing or not?

5. Social media: good or bad?

6. When must we stop blaming our parents?

7. Have you ever dealt with a narcissist? If so, have you been able to free yourself? Why or why not? If you have, how?

8. What character did you most relate to and why?

9. How much of what you believe is taken at other people's word? What does it take for you to be certain about something? How much or how little? Are you naturally skeptical or accepting? Why?

Acknowledgments

With gratitude to Ami McConnell, Daisy Hutton, Janna Reiss, Jodi Hughes, Chip MacGregor, and all those who made a difference and contributed to the making of this book. Much love to you all!

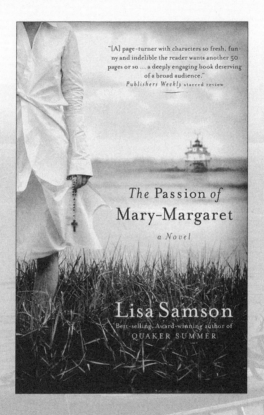

978159554466-D

An Excerpt from

The Passion of Mary-Margaret

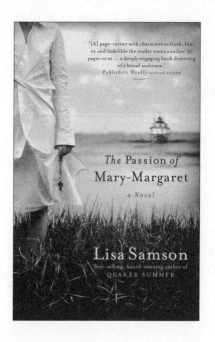

Author's Notes:

1. *The Passion of Mary-Margaret* is not a retelling of Hosea and was not written to be read as such.
2. The term *religious* is used in this work as a noun at times. A "religious" is a priest, a brother, a nun, or a religious sister who is bound by vows to an order or who has received the sacrament of Holy Orders.
3. A religious sister technically is not a nun. A nun is cloistered within the walls of a convent or monastery.

October 2000

Dear Angie,

All these years and it has come to this. You've outlived me. I knew it would happen and I knew you'd be the one to find this in my underwear drawer. Why Mary-Francis had to come up with the idea of writing down our lives for the benefit of those who'll follow us is understandable, but no less annoying. I think anonymity in serving God is crucial to the devout life, so I'm only going to let this be unearthed after my passing. However, I suppose Mary-Francis is right in the long run. We have a history here and it's part of the new sisters' story. We all belong to one another, but that doesn't mean they get to know everything about me while I'm still around. A girl has a right to keep some things to herself. But I do promise to tell this with as much love and grace as I can despite my attitude! (There's service in a nutshell for you.) So you can breathe a little easier, my friend.

I write for those who will follow us, so they'll know that sometimes God calls us to do things we may never understand, and that sometimes God calls us to do things we can grasp the

275

reason of right away. Usually there's a little of both in the mix if you live long enough and develop the capability of recognizing the Divine fingerprint. Holy smudges abound indeed.

I've loved serving God with you. I am in good health as I write the following recollections at seventy years of age, and with Sister Pascal due to arrive in a few months, so young and full of the verve we could all use a little of these days, I thought maybe I should heed Mary-Francis's words. Perhaps we might impart a little of what we've learned even when we're gone. Although, indeed, I've never felt particularly wise, just willing. And even then, my brain sometimes protested like an argumentative Sophomore even though my body jumped in the car and took off. Jesus was always at the wheel, but he's not particularly cautious. In fact, he takes hairpin turns at seventy miles per hour if you want to know the truth of it. But as he is God, I've always figured he knows how to drive better than I do. Yes, I've left myself wide open for a smart-mouthed comment from you. Refrain yourself, missy. I'm not a slowpoke, I'm simply careful. And I'm not the one who had my license suspended when I was twenty, might I remind you. Oh, Angie, we've had fun, haven't we?

You've been my good friend, my companion, and my sister in the faith and in the Lord for so long. And we've eaten a lot of ice cream together too, made big messes in the kitchen, and laughed ourselves silly during the monologues on *The Tonight Show*. Selfishly, I hope you miss me. But you're not much younger than I am; I bet I'll be seeing you soon.

Love always,
Mary-Margaret Fischer, SSSM

P.S. You don't think this will offend anybody, do you? You'll notice I left out the time you, Jude, and I went down to Aruba. Nobody ever needs to know about that, I assure you!

~⌒

*This little collection of my scribblings is dedicated to the School Sisters
of St. Mary's who will follow me in this place. God be with you.
I'm praying for you and shall be until we meet face-to-face.*

*Mary-Margaret Fischer, SSSM,
Abbeyville, Locust Island, Maryland, October 2000*

MY SISTERS, IF I BEGAN THIS TALE AT THE END, YOU WOULD know my heart is full of love even though nothing went as planned. I could tell you God's ways are not ours, but you probably know that already. And I could tell you that his mercy takes shape in forms we cannot begin to imagine, but unless you walked in my shoes for the past seventy years, you could not feel the mercy I have been given. The mercy God gives us is our own to receive, and while sometimes it overlaps with others' like the gentle waves of the bay on the banks of which I now sit, for the most part, the sum and substance of it, the combination of graces, is as unique as we are.

So I will begin this tale at the beginning, on the night my mother conceived me in a moment of evil, a moment not remotely in the will of God, although some might beg to differ on that particular point of theology. It's their right and I don't possess the doctrinal ardor to argue such things anymore. So be it. What you think or what I think on the matter doesn't necessarily make it true. God is as he is and our thoughts do not change him one way or the other. If you've an ounce of intellect, you'll take as much comfort in that as I do.

My mother, Mary Margaret the First, as my grandmother called her, began cradling my life inside of her when a young

278

seminarian took her against her will by the walls of Fort McHenry. Most evenings after teaching second grade in South Baltimore, she walked up Fort Avenue to the five-pointed star-shaped fort from which the Battle of Baltimore was fought in 1814, rockets red glare, bombs bursting in air, and so forth; and those British frigates sailed up the Patapsco River with Francis Scott Key on deck, penning what would become our national anthem.

The seminarian knew about what my Aunt Elfi called my mother's "evening constitutional" and sometimes he would join her in the gaslit, city twilight, hands clasped behind his back—at least I picture him that way—bent a bit forward at the waist and listening to her talk about her students perhaps, maybe the other religious sisters, for she had just taken her final vows as a School Sister of Notre Dame. Perhaps she talked about her pupils' parents, or how she enjoyed listening to the radio shows in the evenings in the cramped apartment she shared with her friend, fellow sister, and coteacher Loreto; how their school had been seeking ways to provide at least one good meal to the children a day, considering how many of their parents were out of a job after the crash on Wall Street.

I don't know what my father must have said in return, but I've always wondered. She must have been caught by surprise, surely, because Grandmom said my mother was sharp and quite a good reader of people. He must have fooled her somehow. Grandmom said he was the seminarian at nearby Holy Cross Church. Perhaps he'd even heard her confessions. Not that they'd have been shocking. Grandmom said my mother didn't give her much trouble.

Perhaps as they walked, the sun slanted its rays against the faces of the buildings, turning the stones and bricks from gold to crimson, the sky blazing with magenta and violet as though sheer scarves were waving behind the clouds. Maybe the cobalt night soaked into their clothing during the chill months, deepening the black of their coats, drawing the color out of their scarves and the character out of their features until they happened by a lamplight.

One evening something evil entered into him and he entered into her and I resulted. Did Grandmom tell me? If so, she certainly didn't employ that terminology. My age necessitated more delicate, obscure phrasing, perhaps something about the things only husbands and wives should do being forced on someone else. I can't recall exactly when I found out, but it feels like something I've always known and preternaturally understood. I might have overheard a conversation. I don't know. That my mother was a religious sister in an unwanted pregnancy threw fate completely out of balance. When I was thirteen, I figured I could put things aright somehow, maybe justify my existence by picking up the torch my own birth snuffed out.

It's bad enough to be born from the sin of two consenting adults. But I resulted from rage and control, from one person overpowering another in the assumption his right to take was more important than her right to give. That takes "man meaning it for evil but God meaning it for good" a giant step further. Yet blaming God for the lies of an Egyptian nobleman's wife who didn't succeed in getting Joseph to succumb to her hardly subtle sexual requests and that wine steward's selfish forgetfulness is somewhat different than giving him wholesale credit for rape. You have to draw the line somewhere or pretty soon Ted Bundy truly couldn't help himself and that terrorist they're talking about these days, Osama Bin Something or Other, really is on a holy mission, and who knows where that will end up? That sort of theology shouldn't sit well with anybody, whether you're from Geneva or Rome, so perhaps I have more doctrinal ardor than I realized ten minutes ago! Goodness me. I suppose I've grown slightly opinionated now that I've entered my eighth decade. So sisters, forgive an old woman a little rambling at times. Not that seventy is *that* old, mind you. Indeed not.

My mother came home to Locust Island to grow a healthy baby inside of her as she strolled by the shore and prayed in the chapel here at St. Mary's, feeling at home among the sisters. My grandmother's house was just down the street from the school. She prayed hours and hours on a kneeler, spending more time on her knees than at home. Aunt Elfi most likely joined her frequently because Aunt Elfi knew being present was the first way of helping anyone.

Grandmom said my mother would sit on Bethlehem Point every evening and stare out over the waters of the Chesapeake, her gaze pinned to the spider-legged lighthouse out on the shoals. And she'd cry. Grandmom didn't ask her to expound or emote. Grandmom was second-generation German. The chill had yet to dissipate completely.

I imagine Mary Margaret the First took hope in that whirling light of the lighthouse out on the shoals, as I always have. It makes me think that somehow there's somebody capable of warning you of danger, and if you find yourself in it, that person will climb into a lifeboat and come to get you. It's difficult to take your eyes off the piercing white beam when you sit here on a dark night.

We all want to be rescued and we'll look in the craziest places for that rescuer, won't we? We all want to be found.

Mary Margaret the First sat beneath the same tree under which I'm sitting now. It's one of the reasons I always end up here. The way the tangled roots protrude from the ground perfectly cradles my lawn chair, and on afternoons in late July or August, the canopy of leaves stifles some of the sun's heat. Only when my mother sat here, it was young, a tree with more hope than wisdom.

Conceived in sin, birthed in sorrow, I entered the world in

a flow of blood that failed to cease once I had been released into my grandmother's hands. After fifteen minutes or so, Grandmom knew the bleeding wouldn't stop on its own; my mother was dying. Aunt Elfi fetched Doctor Spanyer, who said with an aching stutter that by the time they'd deliver my mother to the h-h-hospital, having to procure a boat to the mainland and then ride two hours to Salisbury, she'd be d-d-dead. The poor doctor died a year later on the way to the very place my mother couldn't go, his wife refusing to believe he'd bleed out when his son Marlow ran over his foot with the lawn mower. He did. She moved away after the funeral.

The inhabitants of Locust Island formed a hardy, scrabbly sort of people back then because every person knew in their core that if something traumatic happened physically, the nearest hospital more than two hours away, there was nothing to be done but die. And if death was the only outcome, well, the sooner the better and heaven above let it be something massive and quick: a fall from a roof onto your head, a fatal heart attack or stroke, a smash on the skull with a sledgehammer. A lawn mower accident. Postpartum uterine hemorrhaging.

Aunt Elfi then slipped out into the rain and fetched Father Thomas, our parish priest. Tears in his eyes, for he was my mother's confessor, he anointed my mother's forehead, eyes, ears, nostrils, lips, hands, and feet and prayed the prayers of extreme unction, the first prayers my new ears ever heard. Aunt Elfi said he then picked me up and said, "The final puzzle piece in Mary Margaret's redemption."

I still don't know what that means. I can't say my life is completely explainable, that I don't have a lot of questions. God willing, the answers will be unearthed before I die.

My grandmother named me Mary-Margaret the moment my mother passed away. I've always liked the hyphen she gave, as if somehow it serves as a bridge between my mother and me, a gentle, silent "and so on and so forth." And it is my own hyphen.

Had my mother lived, I most likely would not be writing in this notebook. She planned on giving me up for adoption, wanting me to have both a mother and a father, and returning to her order, teaching, most likely farther away, leaving the entire ordeal behind her. And I wouldn't have blamed her. Of course Grandmom said she always planned to raise me there in the little apartment with one couch and too many straight chairs; that she would never have let me go to another family when ours was well and good and fully capable of raising a child. And I can only believe her as she never did pass me on to anybody else.

The main players in this morality tale have passed on: Jude, my mother, Grandmom and Aunt Elfi, Brister, Petra, Mr. Keller, and even LaBella. Except for John, Gerald, and Hattie, and myself. Actually, if you're reading this, *I* am dead too. I assume the raping seminarian passed away as well. I never knew what happened to him. Who among us would have the spirit to embark on such a search? I don't even know his name, if anyone discovered his crime, or if he slunk away into the arms of the Church.

And did he take refuge in the arms of Christ? Did he seek forgiveness? Did he, perhaps, turn into something more?

See? Questions. Never to be answered. Most likely I've waited too long. He'd be long in his grave by now. *I'm* old!

Well, my Aunt Elfi said my mother's soul passed into me as lightning trilled the air around us. Grandmom said she was crazy, we were all Catholic, we didn't believe in that sort of thing; surely the soul entered the baby well before she was born and would she please be quiet and help her wash her only daughter's body and clean up the blood?

The blood she gave for me. Yes, I'm painfully aware of the symbolism.

Aunt Elfi would have carefully rolled up her sleeves, donned an apron, and pulled back her long, white hair. She would have lovingly dabbed each rose-bloom of blood away, leaving a comet of iron-red across my mother's thighs as she wiped her clean. Aunt Elfi moved in a gentle, patting way, her voice never much above a whisper.

My mother, by the way, was the product of an indiscretion between my twenty-eight-yet-still-unmarried grandmother and an island tourist from Belgium. Though completely out of character for my thick-jawed grandmother, even less understandable was that he found her horsey, Germanic face attractive. So sex seemed to be something unredeemed in and of itself in my family of females, but somehow taken up and looped around the fingers of the Almighty and put to rights in the aftermath.

Well, Aunt Elfi never misbehaved like her sister, but it only took one look at her to realize someone scrambled her brain with a fork before it was fully cooked.

Later on that September afternoon in 1930, the sky clear and the orange sun gilding the fallen rain, men and women walked home from the dock, from their fishing boats or the seafood cannery at the western edge of our island. Cans and cans of oysters were shipped out from Locust Island every day. Abbey Oysters. The company used a monk as the logo even though many of the islanders were Methodists. As you can imagine, Friday was the best day for sales, a fact that did not escape even the most Methodist of Methodists. Sometimes I walked by the cement block building and looked through the grimy window, watching as the shuckers' hands darted like minnows extracting the smooth, precious meat from the rough, prehistoric exterior. Rounding the corner, the pile of shells grew with each day, only to be carted away and ground into lime.

Those men and women passed by, oblivious to the tragedy as they scuffled down Main Street in front of our building.

They didn't know the bell from St. Mary's Convent School that called the girls to dinner served as a death knell for Sister Mary Margaret Fischer as well as a ringing in of a new life, proof, some wise person once said, that God desires the human race to continue. They figured another day had passed, much like the one before and the one before that, back to the day one of their parents or siblings or children passed away or someone was born into this world. We always remember days when something begins or ends.

And as those two women washed the bloody legs and the pale, fragile arms of my mother—pictures of her display lovely, wavy, dark hair and dark eyes—I lay bundled on the bed, looking up at the ceiling. That's what Aunt Elfi told me. I didn't cry until Father Thomas returned to comfort us in our sorrow and he gathered me into his fragile arms, crying with me. He was a tender sort until the day he passed away.

I was two days old when Father Thomas, the older members of our parish, and our family, consisting of my grandmother, my aunt, and myself, committed my mother to the earth at St. Francis Church's graveyard. Afterward, they walked right inside the church, stood by the simple, stone baptismal font, and I was baptized in the name of the Father and the Son and the Holy Spirit. Sister Thaddeus, whom I'll tell you more about later, an older schoolgirl at the time, said she watched from the shadows, listening to the Holy Spirit telling her to pray for me every day. And she did.

Afterward, Aunt Elfi brought me to Bethlehem Point, this very piece of land on which I now sit, beneath the same tree, and she held me as the sun went down for good over my mother. She walked back home with me in her arms, fed me a bottle, and laid me in my bassinette, where I slept through the night. Exhausted, they both deserved that little ray of grace. I never gave them any trouble either.

SO, MY SISTERS, I FIGURE I'LL TELL YOU WHAT'S GOING ON these days while I jot down this little history, that way if something of note happens to me, this is all recorded and I won't have to scrape my brain to locate the information. I can tell you what happened forty years ago with little problem, but last week sits somewhere between the equation for finding the angles of an isosceles triangle and the name of the main character in *Breakfast at Tiffany's*. Am I killing two birds with one stone or robbing Peter to pay Paul by doing it this way? Feel free to be the judge of that.

Earlier today Sister Angie (given name Angelica) opened a blue and green webbed folding chair and set it beside mine. We've been together a long time. My mother's sugar maple tree blared that beautiful orange-red. Sugar maples get a bit braggy in the fall.

"What's in your lap?" She pointed to this notebook open to the passage you just read, my pen resting in the fold.

"Just writing down some memories."

She sat in her chair, stretched her legs straight out in front of her, and folded her hands atop her tummy. "Mary-Francis is on my case too. I need to get moving, I guess."

I agreed. During Angie's years as a school sister, she was

surrounded by a pack of wild dogs in a remote school in Alaska, was chased by revolutionaries in South America, and picnicked in France with rich schoolgirls. Angie was even arrested down at the School of the Americas, but that has nothing to do with our order. She's just an upstart when she finds the time. She taught in eight different schools and we ended up back here together at St. Mary's. She lived the life I thought I was going to. (Right, Angie? Yes, I can see you rolling your eyes.)

She adjusted the back of her chair, setting the teeth of the arms to recline a little. "I went to see Gerald and Hattie a few minutes ago," she said.

"How's Gerald doing?" I snapped shut this notebook and slid it into my tote bag.

"Not well. Hattie's so upset about his condition they had to give her a light sedative. But she told me that Gerald had something to tell you and to get on over there." Angie leaned forward and whispered, though no one else was around. "She said you wouldn't like it in the long run. She said it was about your mother when push came to shove."

My mother?

I stared at the old lighthouse out in the bay off the southern point of the island. Hattie and Gerald lived there for years, the last lightkeepers on the Chesapeake Bay. If you are reading this, I hope you've come, or will come, to love these waters as much as I always have. They are like a mother to me, the home to which I've always returned eventually. Jude would have gone crazy out on the waters had he lived there all those years like his older brother, Gerald; this island made him crazy enough.

Oh and by the way, this is Jude's story as well. You cannot hear mine without hearing his.

The light circled around inside the plastic lens. The great Fresnel lens, an artistic, graceful beehive of beveled glass, was smashed years earlier by a baseball bat held in Jude's hands.

Jude's soul frothed and foamed, stirred by an anger that began fermenting well before the day his mother left the light and took him with her. But I don't want to get ahead of myself. Jude and I had mother issues in common, indeed. Most likely, it drew us together. Unfortunately, back then, Jude was wont to concentrate on the mercies he thought he was *denied*.

"Poor Gerald. The last of the Keller men." I waved to Glen Keesey sailing by in his Sunfish. Glen waved back and held up his book, my copy of *Bluebeard*. Between March and November, Glen sails out to Hathaway Island, a small, uninhabited, marshy speck half a mile east of the light, so he can sunbathe in the buff. He joins us for a glass of wine every once in a while too, while we watch the sunset.

"Yep. All gone but Gerald." Angie nodded, removing a barrette from her hair and replacing it, retightening the entire arrangement. Her knuckles have become knobby, but she always keeps her nails so nice. She's prissy. Tough, but prissy. I've rarely seen her without some makeup, and her shoes, while comfortable, are never ever called sensible. "It's the end of an era, Mary."

The sisters all call me Mary. Mary-Margaret's a mouthful.

She looked upon the lighthouse too, a structure that seemed somehow less for all the automation going on inside. Aunt Elfi used to say that people dignify most structures, enliven them. Without us, what is the need? If you think I'm wrong, just imagine nobody ever going up and down the Eiffel Tower again. And why do ruins make us yearn to go live there?

I pointed to the lighthouse. "Mr. Keller saved many a life. Hard to believe the place is empty."

She harrumphed. "I'm sure the ghost of Mr. Keller got back there somehow. I think that lighthouse was the only thing he ever really loved."

Angie and I differ on what Mr. Keller should have done

when his wife, Jude's mother, contracted cabin fever. I say he couldn't have possibly known what was going on. She says any man worth his salt should have figured all was not right, that he had to have known somewhere deep in his soul something was horribly wrong with his wife.

"I'll see to Hattie." I stood and lifted the straps of my canvas tote up onto my shoulder, trying to shove those heavy thoughts aside.

"It would be a good idea. She needs you."

So I gathered my chair and traipsed through the tall brown grasses of early October toward St. Mary's Village Assisted Living. After Grandmom died of a heart attack, I went to live there at the age of eight. It was a convent school back then; Aunt Elfi moved to a monastery in Tibet hoping they'd be more amenable to her odd religious juxtapositions, hoping to find something resembling Shangri La, which she never stopped talking about after reading *Lost Horizon*. Although I knew how much she loved me, this didn't come as a surprise to me. Even I knew my grandmother cared for Aunt Elfi every bit as much as she cared for me.

I passed the entrance of the old drugstore—now a gamer café—where I first spent time with Jude, and I looked back at Bethlehem Point Light and, because I believed it only fitting and proper, prayed for those who once lived inside its walls.

It's late now and time for sleep.

The story continues in *The Passion of Mary-Margaret* by Lisa Samson.

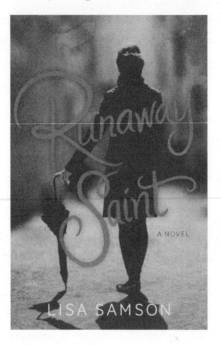

Being married to a saint isn't what it's cracked up to be.

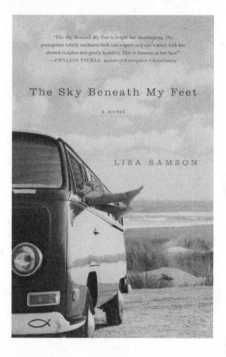

"*The Sky Beneath My Feet* is bright but unassuming. The protagonist totally enchants both one's spirit and one's mind with her shrewd insights and gentle humility. This is Samson at her best!"

—PHYLLIS TICKLE, AUTHOR OF *EMERGENCE CHRISTIANITY*

Available in print and e-book

THOMAS NELSON
Since 1798

A STRANGE AND WONDROUS
FRIENDSHIP IGNITES THE FIRE OF
LOVE IN MAY SEYMOUR'S LIFE.

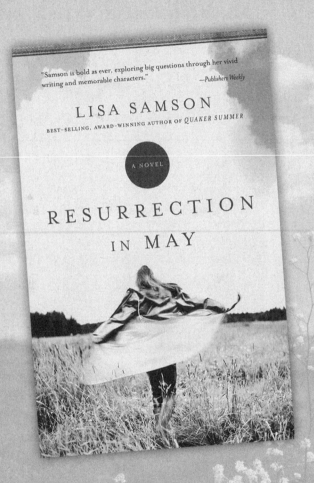

"Samson is bold as ever, exploring big questions through her vivid
writing and memorable characters."
—*Publishers Weekly*

LISA SAMSON

BEST-SELLING, AWARD-WINNING AUTHOR OF *QUAKER SUMMER*

A NOVEL

RESURRECTION
IN MAY

Available in print and e-book

THOMAS NELSON
Since 1798

Biting and gentle, hard-edged and hopeful
. . . a beautiful fable of love and power, hiding
and seeking, woundedness and redemption.

EMBRACE ME

believing is seeing

From the Acclaimed Novelist of *Quaker Summer*
LISA SAMSON

Available in print and e-book

THOMAS NELSON
Since 1798

Sometimes you have
to go a little bit CRAZY to find the
life you were meant to live.

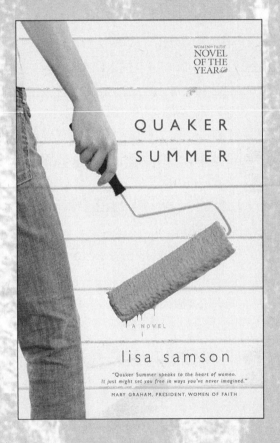

Available in print and e-book

THOMAS NELSON
Since 1798

About the Author

Lisa Samson lives in Kentucky. She has three children and enjoys art and making good food. She is the author of 35 books, a two-time recipient of the *Christianity Today* novel of the year award, a Christy Award winner, and grateful for all she has been given. You can find her on Facebook at writerlisasamson.Facebook: Lisa-Samson